SUEÑO *EN* *LLAMAS*
from the Ashes His Conscience was Born

Marvin DeLos Reyes

Content

¡...Alumbra, lumbre de alumbre
Luzbel de piedralumbre!

Miguel Ángel Asturias

Chapter 1
He wants to save his memory before the flames destroy it.

A dark thick cloud obscures his vision and scorches his throat. He swallows smoke. He swallows sorrow. He swallows his own memory submerged in the gush of salty water dripping from his forehead drowning desperate shouts. These heart-rending cries pierce his eardrums like needles spearing a voodoo doll. What sorcerer conducts this damn ceremony? What sin do the flames approaching his frightened eyes wish to purify? For a moment he's completely mesmerized by the spits of flame that dash against the ceiling and splash the paintings that embellish the walls with vestiges of the Old World. The walls, blackened by a blow of coal dust, darken his vision and everyone crumples and everyone screams. Everyone steps on the terrified child curled up in a forgotten corner just waiting for this ceremony to end. Then, through the bolted metal bars blocking the window, he sees the child and extends his hand. He wants to help him. He wants to help himself. He wants to save his memory before the flames destroy it. And all of a sudden, a scream, an explosion, the room reverberates, the dream crumbles... once again the alarm clock has saved his life.

When will the flames finally stop burning his dreams? And who is that child lying on the sacrificing stone bed waiting for his turn? Why does this dream continue hunting him? How is it that this dream, which began when he was a child showing him a simple still frame of flames, throughout the years had become a scene of horror that returns again and again? Why? Why? If he'd been more thorough, he would've noticed that the dreams intensified as the end of January approached. But, much like everyone else, he remained oblivious to the signs that life offers to solve the puzzle.

He did notice that lately the dreams had revealed more details about the sinister act. Even though he'd never been able to see the child's face, this time he'd felt the boy's anguish and desperation more fully. Was it possible that time was reminding him of something he'd pawned in the past? So many people had tried to climb up to the attic of his memory guided by the lantern of truth but they'd found the door blocked by old furniture dusted with a history that didn't belong to him. Soon he'll discover that the flames were sparked by ghosts created in one of the most brutal historic episodes of the land that had seen him be born after the other. Until then, this Nazarene would have to be satisfied accompanying his cross over hills until the procession ended. An end that was indeed where everything had begun.

* * *

While the cold sweat of the nightmare chills his skin, the Latino radio station plays an Arjona song. The lyrics echo in the room but he, like most listeners, doesn't pay attention. This message, like so many denunciations that use music to evoke change, would be lost in the shades of the forgetfulness... "*Vapulearon a otro indocumentado*, Another undocumented alien was beat up / *fue en defensa propia*, it was in self-defense / *dijeron los del jurado*, concluded a jury of "his" peers..." He rises and his semi-rigid manhood shows him the way to the shower. He is agile, fit, dark-skinned and short. His chin is speckled with an eternally millimetric beard that refuses to grow and that matches his pubes. He'd begun trimming down there over the summer while he'd still been in high school.

Everything began by pure physical necessity. When it had finally been his turn to go out with a girl with a reputation that was a "little stained" and interesting fetishes, she'd told him, *"Yo no tengo pelos en la lengua.* I do not have hair on my tongue," accompanied with a wink. At first he thought she was referring to the Spanish version of telling it like it is but no, she had meant it literally. After a thorough ten second deliberation (which might have been five), he'd decided he would prefer to look like a plucked chicken than go to bed every night with the sheets as high as a circus tent. Without further ado, the thick black bush was shaved. He had discovered how sensual that region becomes once ridded of its shield and how easy the oils of desire run thereafter, sufficient reasons to continue the morning ritual. That fall he discovered in the showers after PE that his Kama Sutra tutor had managed to pluck almost everyone in his class.

While he bathes and the foam surfs down his hard body, he considers what he'll do after receiving his Master's Degree in Filmmaking. He was pretty sure he would continue working with el Waldo and la Tere. Perhaps then the muse would finally visit Waldo and he would finish the ever so-dragging script. He wanted so much to finally be able to shoot his first movie. And maybe, just maybe then he would exorcise the demons that prevented him from catching any decent sleep. Wetting everything nearby, he got out and dried his hair, oblivious to la Tere's admiration of his sex as it swung like pendulum from four to six.

"Mrs. Robinson, you're trying to seduce me. Aren't you?" She displayed her bright, beautiful smile.

Shocked and embarrassed, he tried to cover himself. "Mierda Tere, at least you should've told me you were coming over."

"If you weren't always in the clouds, you would of remembered that yesterday we agreed we'd scout the location for the commercial."

"Oh crap! You're right." She turned around but peeked at the reflection in the window. He got dressed as quickly as he had always done whenever a mother had unlocked the door of her daughters' room while they were studying.

"I'm sorry, it just that--"

"You had a bad dream," she concluded, knowing what he'd been about to say. "You should really go see my dad. He'll help you with that. You can't just keep having that horrible dream. You know exactly how it's affecting you."

"How can your dad help me if he still has nightmares about Fidel and the Bay of Pigs?"

"Don't you dare tell him that! He'd lose it!"

"Don't worry, I'm just kiddin'. OK, you can turn around now."

She turned around and feigned surprise. "Oh you're dressed. Well, I hope your good mood lasts through the day cuz we've gotta talk to the client and we're already running late. Hurry! We still got to pick up Waldo."

"Waldo's not gonna be ready. You'll see. Alright, let's go!" He pushed her through the door.

"So you still carry the mark ah?" she asked.

"What d'you mean?"

"The mark of the plucked ones." She smiled.

"Just go, alright. We're already late!" he said to brush off his embarrassment.

* * *

Waldo lived in the same Barrio his parents had emigrated to after leaving Nicaragua when he'd been a child. The three had met in high school. Ishto's curiosity had been stirred because Waldo had been the only one not plucked that summer, so he'd asked about it straight out. In that simple way, a friendship that would span their entire lives had begun. That same fall he'd met Tere, who had been assigned by her girlfriends to investigate The Plucking Case. She'd always been drawn to intriguing subjects.

Destiny united them. Since then they'd worked together on almost everything. For a while they helped out at the bodega owned by don Pedro, Waldo's dad. Don Pedro had come to the States with a backpack full of dreams, his head full of muses and his pockets full of air. His hard work cleaning offices might have scared away his muses--although in a forgotten drawer he still keeps his best shot at being a writer-- but it paid off when he brought over doña Rosita and their offspring. After many more years of sacrifices, they had finally achieved the American dream. The naming of la bodega "Margarita" was a tribute to Dario's poem, his favorite poet, and to his mother who had died long before the hated dynasty collapsed. He always made sure that people understood that the tribute didn't extend to the person who had inspired the poem. To his eyes, everything and everyone related to that family didn't deserve anything from him or anybody else.

Waldo lived on the store's second floor and woke every morning to the scent of the bread that had just left the oven. Latinos, especially the ones from Centro America, couldn't stand not having freshly baked bread every morning. Perhaps drawn by the scent of fresh bread or by Waldo's sensitivity, the muses that had abandoned don Pedro returned to flirt with his son. He'd been writing for some time but had never dared to show his writings to anyone. Instead he kept anonymously hunting new stories. Without knowing it, he was already part of one himself.

When Ishto and Tere arrived, Waldo was outside finishing up a *hojaldra*, a sweet bread. As he got into the car he said, "Late, as usual." He looked at Tere, assuming she had made Ishto late.

"Hey, wait a minute! Don't look at me. I'm always on time."

"It was el Ishto, then." He eyed Ishto's reflection in the rearview mirror.

Ishto simply said, "Latino's time, bro', Latino's time."

"Yeah, right." Tere looked for the correct address. "Does anyone know where we're going?"

"Don't worry," Waldo said. "I know, *andare dritto.*"

"What?"

"*Andare dritto, baboso.* Just keep going straight, man. *Che Dio abbia pieta' della vostra anima.*"

Ishto and Tere were used to Waldo's eccentricities so they looked at each other and laughed.

"Yeah, keep laughing", Waldo said. "Anyway, you *Chapines* only understand what's of your convenience."

"And sometimes not event that, bro'," Ishto answered.

La Tere kept applying makeup. She was *coqueta,* that Spanish word almost impossible to translate that describes the essence of Latinas, the word vain doesn't begin to convey. Her beauty, the result of a Mexican-Cuban mixture, allowed her to be that and more...much more. Her Mexican roots provided pitch-black hair and her white complexion came from the Cuban bourgeois before the Revolution. She had inherited an analytical sense from her dad, and from her mother...who knew?, Her mom had died when Tere was still a child.

"When are you going to finish putting all that stuff on you face, Tere?" Ishto asked.

"Leave her alone, man! Remember that the only reason we got this gig was because la Tere was flirting with the client," Waldo said.

"Well, if you did your job as a writer, we wouldn't have to rely on those crafts."

"It's not my fault my scripts are too sophisticated for their minds." Waldo pulled out the pocket notebook that always escorted him. "I already told you man, these people like simple stuff. If it were up to them, I would end up shooting *culos,* asses, even in food commercials, dude. Don't you see that's what they want? We have to give them what they want!"

"Oh, that's the place", la Tere said.

"Leave the metaphor locked in the car," Ishto said. "Just talk to them easy, plain language man, OK?"

Waldo's eyes were fixed in the faces of the *jornaleros,* day laborers, in front of a Seven Eleven.

"Waldo? Waldo!"

Waldo did not respond. He had already disappeared into his writings.

Chapter 2
The *Jornalero*

Walking through the intersection of Solitude and Reminiscence, the *jornalero,* feels like a newborn after the umbilical cord has been severed: without connections, without roots, without that something that joins him to an elusive and foreign place. It's a bit past eight o'clock in the evening and although he's tired, he's happy because today he was one of the lucky ones. He was one of the *jornaleros* chosen by the mister who, wiser than Salomon, day in and day out selected those with the greatest need to work for a mere pittance and be grateful for the exploitation. At the end is win/win...or lose/lose, depending on whom you ask.

He continues walking towards his house...apartment...buildin'... whatever you want to call it. It doesn't matter; the only thing that matters is that it's not home. His true home, modest and humble, was left behind much like the green forest of his little town and the *rancho,* hut, neither of which he had to share with strangers who use expressions he doesn't understand. It never bothered him to sleep on the uneven floor, on that worn-out *petate,* mat, alongside his brothers because they were flesh and blood. But these people...they only tried to take advantage of the new roommate.

"We're all brothers and sisters, *Raza!* We must stand united! That's the only way we'll achieve something in this great country!" proclaim the Latino politicians from the tiny black-and-white television that every night became the light that fascinated the moths with its images. If they would only leave their offices at the Capitol, they would know how different things are down here. Down here, we eat each other alive, he thought. But perhaps they did know that, especially in election year when they––Elephants or Donkeys––did the same thing to each other. The only difference is that they did it wearing Giorgio Armani.

He walks by a McDonald's. *Tengo hambre, I'm hungry.* This feeling triggers the internal fight: If I eat today, what about tomorrow? What tomorrow? There might be no tomorrow. They say the gringos are trying to kick us all in the ass and send us back to the very same places where they for many years negotiated many lives to save us from Communism. He continues walking.

He passes a store and hears a commercial from a Spanish radio station selling prepaid calling cards "to be close to the ones you love." Among the numbers advertised only three stick in his mind: 1...8...7..., three digits that mean nothing unless you're an illegal immigrant in a land whose sounds you don't understand.

He just keeps walking. He buys a soda so the gaseous bubbles will fill up his stomach much like hope fills up his heart: beaten by the rejection of those who don't look like him.

He arrives. His usual *"Buenas noches, good evening"* doesn't find a response. Of course not, why would it? Not when those who have nothing are every evening hypnotized by the *telenovela,* soap opera, and its images of the utopia they covet. Somehow he squeezes by past the others who share the misery of that crowded apartment. How many? No one knows. Not even the one who signed the lease knows; he limits himself to collecting the rent the last week of the month and always forgets to put in his share. Whenever one leaves, two arrive.

The walls, marked with stains and graffiti, portray their surrealist life and guide him down the hall to the bathroom. He looks for the drawing of the little ship that navigates in his memory, the little ship that will carry him away from here, much like the one --was first tattooed and then drawn-- freed a character from one of the multiple tales his late *abuela,* his grandma, used to tell him. But he doesn't find it. He takes a deep breath before entering the bathroom. Once inside he'll try to breathe the stench-filled air as little as possible.

How he misses his *rancho* in Río Negro! Little, yes; humble, absolutely; but at least spotless. Its dirt floor was always swept clean by the one he left behind and whose love he needs as much as this economy needs the illegals to function. He wants a shower but the sticky green scum in the tub discourages him. Discouragement has interwoven so much of his life he no longer pays attention to it. He gets in. After the sound of a rusty faucet, much like a rat's scream, freezing water cascades over his body. Finally he feels...alive, or at least that he exists.

As the water runs over his body he remembers the waterfall that powered the hydroelectric Chixoy dam and the spot where he and his cousins found a lifeless body sprawled on the ground. He wraps his arms around his body and holds himself tight but his body feels lifeless. He touches himself here and there but it's as if he's touching somebody else's body. Perhaps the broken mirror held together by Scotch tape is right. Perhaps that's the only object that sees him as he truly is. A man broken into three pieces: the past, the present, and the future; what he was, what he is, what he will be; what he wanted to be, what he wants to be, what he will want to be——all welded together by a fire that gutters day after day, extinguished every second by that thing called reality.

He keeps touching his body to convince himself that he's still the same or to convince himself otherwise. That...that used to wake up to the slightest touch, today remains wrapped in slumber. Why would it want to wake? Back-breaking work and worries have killed its desire. Perhaps he's much like it and wants to keep on sleeping and pretending he's somewhere else. Perhaps he wants to keep dreaming he's home at the annual fair in his *pueblo*, town, with the smell of caramel candy, the sounds of the *lotería,* games of chance, and the noise of firecrackers going off just a few feet away from him... bam!... bam!... bam!... bam!..

The knocks at the door bring him back to reality. There's always someone who needs to use the bathroom, there's always someone who brings him back to see what he refuses to see. He steps back into the murkiness of the surrounding world.

It's pitch black inside. Outside the streetlight illuminates the young girl who sells her body for a few measly dollars. The glow barely filters through the cracks in the windows but it's enough to make out the silhouettes of bodies in perfect *chiaroscuro* on the floor: sleeping, dreaming, or simply escaping reality. He has witnessed this scene before. He has seen bodies scattered on the ground but those had been stained with their own blood. This scene reminds him of American films that try to recreate what he lived, impeccably lit by a director of photography who utilizes the aesthetics of film to tell the story historians left out, perhaps to bring about justice, perhaps to bring about closure, or perhaps simply because war movies are big at the box office and make Hollywood studios millions. (Unfortunately this is not one of those films and not even I, who write this story, can create a Hollywood ending.)

The couple in the far corner has gone off to satisfy their carnal urges, which will keep him awake for at least another half hour. The adolescents in the other corner will vicariously satisfy their own listening to the couple's desperate lovemaking. Soon the air would be filled with the smell of semen and sweat, and the how-the-fuck-did-I-get-here scream will once again get caught in his throat.

They finally finish their acrobatic lovemaking, the bump and grind of bodies in heat. Now the shout of police sirens remind him that he no longer lives in the countryside, that he's just another illegal from the *campo,* countryside, living in a big city. Yes, this is the city and noise never stops. Tomorrow will be another day and he'll have to pray to once again be one of the few chosen for exploitation. Tomorrow the other day laborers out on University Boulevard will tell him that Chucho, the one with the sick son back home, took off with a stranger who smiled a lot, drove a brand new car and wore skintight clothes.

And he would know then that when desperation attacks, pride surrenders. And he will wonder when it will be his turn. And he'll sit down and wait, then he'll wait some more, and at the end of the day all he'll end up with will be a photo of himself in a folder named "The Day Laborers" in the files of the Minutemen and again he'll lose himself in this world full of people who keep looking for their place in the land of opportunity without realizing they'd already found it. And he'll dream and while dreaming he'll rise to the sky and from there he'll understand that it's better to die with his own people than to starve surrounded by foreigners in the land of the uncle who loves you and takes care of you as long as someone here has cut your umbilical cord.

Chapter 3
One After the Other had been Born

Holding the two *patojos,* boys, by their hands plus balancing the basket of dirty clothes on her head atop a padded ring called a *yagual* was a feat. But all the women managed it. Their hips, wrapped with the red *corte,* an indigenous skirt decorated with yellow lines that meandered over the cloth like rivers, swung as they carefully stepped around the stones in the path. Here women nurtured the children while husbands gathered what the Earth birthed. This way of life would continue unchanged until the children were old enough to endure the arduous fieldwork.

The boys clinging to her *corte* were not hers but she treated them as if they had issued from her womb. They were all that war and destiny had left her. She saw in them the son who had disappeared two years ago and the daughter-in-law *Tata Dios,* God, had taken away just when these children with her now had wailed the first cry of life barely six years ago. One after the other had been born. The midwife had warned them about the twins ahead of time but since these were the first twins in the family, they were viewed with a certain admiration. They are *igualitos,* they're so much alike, people said around town.

The hard work that would have broken another's back made her stronger. She, much like all the women in town, kept home. She was old but that didn't prevent her from performing her duties as leader of the house; thus it had been since her husband died from a stomachache. Despite her loss, she'd raised her only son and saw him marry before bringing his wife home. Together the family had awaited the birth of their children.

The daily routine was hard. Even before the sun was born each morning, she had already ground maize to make tortillas. Before her *nietecitos,* grandchildren, stretched themselves awake on the *petate,* bedroll, she'd already warmed up the black bean soup that would ensure they did not go to the harvest with an empty belly. Every morning Chuz arrived to take them to work and he wouldn't bring them back until *Tata Dios* took the sun away. While they worked the Earth, she wove stories in *güipiles,* the indigenous blouses that would be sold during the weekend *mercado,* market, at the plaza outside the town's church.

Torrential rains had washed the region the previous day, so nobody worked the Earth and the children enjoyed the break. While she washed and dried clothes, they ran and dove in the river with the other children. She let them be young; she tried her best not to let hard work completely consume their childhood. The women slapped their *cortes* and *güipiles* on rocks washed by the river. The river was brave but not more than this indigenous culture that survived in spite of it all.

The day was pretty and sunny. Had the One who would send the tragedy chosen the wrong day? If He had sent it the day before, perhaps everyone would have understood. But today, such a fine day? Why today when everything seems so perfect?

Chapter 4
He saw Himself as a Writer

Looking out of his second-floor bedroom at groups of Latinos that went and came, he thought about the need for someone to tell the stories each one of them had brought in their backpacks over the border. Not as the newspapers or politicians would but as they would by someone who lives among them and whose *latinidad* ran in his own veins. Smelling the aromas of Latin food and listening to salsa tunes flying through the window of this small bedroom overwhelmed with books, he thought that for anyone who called himself a true writer, this would have been reason enough to begin the task. Nevertheless he continued thinking more and writing less.

All his life he'd lived in this barrio in Columbia Pike fifteen minutes from the capital of the most powerful nation on earth, a gap between the First and Third Worlds that had inspired many great writers. Somehow the muses would flirt but never go home with him. Just moments earlier the girl with whom he'd sweated off the fever of passion had said, "You're a writer, tell me something pretty."

Her breasts rubbed like soft peaches against what little hair covered his bony chest. Still dripping sweat and barely having caught his breath, he found a distinct lack of inspiration. He chose to plagiarize one of the great ones and simply said, *"Me gustas cuando callas porque estás como ausente.* I like you when you're quiet 'cuz you're like absent."

Lacking sensitivity or knowledge of poetic greatness but with beautiful perfect body, the girl jumped up. She'd showed similar grace when climbing atop him to ride together towards the glory, flaunted her shining buttock and said, "Don't you ever tell me to shut up!"

He, used to misunderstandings and fleeting loves, thought perhaps it had been for the best. If this beautiful creature didn't spark his creativity, perhaps it was not for him. When she left with her hair still showing signs of their horizontal dance, he murmured to himself, "*Si la vida es un sueño,* if life is a dream, as Lorca claimed, I want to continue dreaming with you."

Despite all this, he considered himself a writer. Their friends said if that was what he wanted, he should go for it. And go for it he did. He'd entered Language and Foreign Studies at American University (AU) because their Spanish department's focus in Latin American Literature was one of the best. He didn't want people to teach him how to write. He wanted to dissect the writings. Semester after semester, he enjoyed the studies. Although he found a few professors who didn't know how to teach and some students who didn't want to learn, he also found teachers who loved the vocation intensely. He located a professor who opened the doors to the wonderful world of Spanish Literature. This compatriot of the founder of Macondo made him understand the concept behind *"las verdades mentirosas y las mentiras verdaderas,"* "The facts hidden in the fiction, and the fiction hidden in the facts." With this she'd awaken the curiosity of he who wanted to write but who didn't know how or even why.

This professor became his mentor, unknowingly materializing a character from Borges' writings, those who search for their destiny without wanting it and who find it without knowing it. He went on to discover Cortázar, Neruda, Monterroso, Asturias, Garcia Márquez, Fuentes, Vargas Llosa, Allende, Monteforte Toledo, and so many more who made him understand that literature is critical to the human being and especially for the Latino. It allows him to rise above reality; to reach a degree of maturity superior to that of those surrounding him.

Ideas, ideas, ideas...how he loved shaping them on pieces of paper that remained hidden. He didn't dare show anybody. He was like the fly that dreamed it was an eagle. But as always, this reflection was truncated because he had to write a stupid commercial for cash to chip in at home, perhaps buy a book, and even invite a girl to catch a movie. Oh well, he thought, at least now I have a pretty phrase I can recycle.

He detested having to write commercials for local stations but thought that the discipline acquire by meeting deadlines would help in the long run. Besides he enjoys working next to his soul siblings and that made everything seem OK. They encouraged him to join their video production classes. He'd refused because according to him once an idea is processed through the lens of a video camera, it loses its purity.

Simple Waldo, simple, Ishto had told him for the commercial's script before dropping him in front of his parent's bodega. He hated it when Ishto said that but commercials, especially those directed to their community, had to be simple. Plus the proprietor of the store had to have his on-camera time and since he most likely did not speak Spanish but pretended to, the text had to be simple and without the alveolar, vibrant, sonorous sound of the double r.

Outside immigrants from all parts of Latin America passed by with their stories covering their faces like a skimask. Inside Waldo continued looking for a story, so immersed in the art he ended up oblivious to it. Downstairs his parents continued nurturing the bodega that, after much sacrifice and in spite of Reaganomics, had managed to stay afloat. His mom, doña Rosita, was in charge and his dad, don Pedro, helped on weekends. During the week he drove their cleaning company employees to wherever they were required.

Every summer since Waldo had been in high school, he'd earned money working for his dad. Then, when he'd met Ishto and Tere, they formed a group in charge of a building. That income had allowed Ishto to buy the digital video camera used to record the commercials and how Waldo had bought his laptop. Tere worked double functions. She was the public relations guru, making friendships everywhere and promoting the business through them; she was also the accountant because of her head for numbers.

Having someone to direct, someone to write and someone to maintain the quota of reality, on a Sixth of January they founded DeLos Reyes Productions. From the beginning the business flourished. And thus this new generation of immigrants, member of Generation Y, began to savor the American dream. Don Pedro helped by describing the benefits of promoting businesses on television to his friends. After years in the area displaying his warmth and openness had made him many friends.

Don Pedro had been the same while he'd still lived in his native country, the land of poets. There he had met Rosa, a Salvadorian immigrant living in Nicaragua. Waldo had been conceived there. It was there too that he'd been slandered and called a *subversivo,* subversive, a death sentence in the Somoza Hacienda. With pain dripping around him he'd left his land during the 1970s. He required four months to cross the bridge between the heart and the progress. He arrived beat-up but excited about building a new life in *el Norte.* Five years later he brought over his beloved Rosita and their son. At that moment, his smile had brightened and his spirit grew stronger. After many acrobatics, he obtained the coveted legal status. Ever since, he'd kept two little flags pinned next to the heart. Waldo, who didn't know his own parents story, continued begging for other people's stories.

Chapter 5
The Street Children

He arrived at the bus terminal depot on a mattress made out of newspapers and layers of coffee with his mouth full of tamarind. He didn't know exactly what had happened. He had jumped into the back of the truck scared for his life. Their usual plan was to flee to the mountain and wait until they'd left. But there hadn't been any warning this time. The truck, his refuge while he was being hunted, had been parked in the outskirts of the village. The engine started and the truck carried him to the capital.

Loud voices and blasts hummed like wasps in the ears. He was no longer in his village. When the gate of the truck opened, he fell to the cold asphalt next to a pile of sugar cane. *"Y vos qué hacés aquí?* What are you doing here? You're one of those thieves here in the terminal, aren't you? *A la mierda, cerote,* go to hell you piece of shit!"

He grabbed a handful of tamarind...the hunger was stabbing his stomach...and ran. There were so many buses and so many people and so much chaos he just sat on the sidewalk and cried. People pushed him aside with their feet. A woman of wide hips adorned by an apron of many layers that danced while joggling a basket of bread on her head told him, *"Mirá vos ishto,* look kid, if you're just sitting there crying, why don't you move over there so you don't bother no one?"

As if blowing a kiss, she pointed with lips stained with an exaggerated red at an abandoned store whose owners had given up after being the victims of who knew how many assaults. There, seated beneath the graffiti signature of the *mara* governing the area, was a boy laughing wildly while his eyes looked for something lost in his memory and his nose sought the madding aroma of a bottle full of carpenter's glue. Others nearby awaited their turn. He moved closer but the older kid kicked him away. There was not enough elixir for anyone else. He moved away.

At the main market between bites of tamarind he witnessed the perfected strategy of children who robbed *jocotes*, Red Mombin, for lunch. While one, perhaps the quickest, distracted the owner, the other took whatever he could and ran off. The runner shouted, "Don't just stand there! Help me! *Picale!*"

He hurled the tamarind and with hands now full of *jocotes* ran with his partner through endless streets. As soon as they arrived at the church, out of breath and with most of the fruits crushed in their hands, the kid who had distracted the vendor complained about having waited longer than usual.

"What happened, *vos cerote?* I thought you bailed on me."

"No, *vos Cascara,* what happened was that I had to go around the other way *vos*. It's fucking crazy with all the *chontes,* police, and shit."

"And this one?"

"I dunno, *vos,* but he helped me carry the *jocotes.*"

"Just give me my share and let's go. We still have to go pick up the newspapers to sell and shit and you know how the fucking Mono, Monkey gets when we're late."

The little one, with a few squashed tamarinds in his pocket, followed them without knowing why.

At the landfill buzzards glided around sweeping mountains of trash in search of some gift from the *Mano Blanca*, the White Hand. Some children harvest the garbage looking for entrees. The kids, accustomed to this world, walked until they reached the *covacha,* hut without having left a trace. El Cascara stopped and said, "Now is your turn, Tripa."

"What the fuck? I went yesterday, *vos.*"
"Yes, but el Mono wasn't there yesterday, so that one doesn't count."
"Hell no! It's not my fault I got lucky, *vos.*"
"Why don't we send him?"
They glanced at the little one. *"Puta vos,* don't be an ass. He doesn't know shit."
"Well, he's gonna have to learn, *maje.*"
"Just go already. I swear if we don't finish selling the fucking paper, I'll tell el Mono it was your fault."

El Cascara pushed around the rag curtain that separated the garbage of the outside from the waste of the inside. El Tripa stayed outside with his new companion and sighed, "I hope he's not horned up." Fifteen minutes passed before el Cascara came out wiping his sticky hands on a page from a newspaper proclaiming the advances obtained by the UNICEF/Government coalition against child abuse. He also carried a package of the afternoon's edition they would try to sell.

Making up headlines because they didn't know how to read, they easily sold newspapers. The little one learned fast and, by dint of his smile, sold his share. At the end of the day they had sold nearly every copy. It was time to give the accounts. They got back to the *covacha* after looking for treasures in the mountains of garbage left by trucks servicing exclusive residential suburbs, they found the others playing dice by the light of a *veladora*, a candle, near the image of the black Christ of the Candelaria.

El Mono rose from the *catre*, mattress, where he left sleeping one of the children who that morning had inhaling fantasies from a bottle. He approached the table where they stood with more desire to flee than to stay. El Mono wore stained blue trousers and a sleeveless t-shirt that revealed the origin of his nickname. "And this one?" he asked.

"El Tripa found him."

"Does he know how to work?"

"He sold as much as we did."

"And what about the other kind of work?"

El Tripa ignored the question. "Here's the money."

They hurled the money onto the table. After counting it, El Mono gave what he believed was fair. They took what they believed was unfair and went to a corner of the *covacha*.

"And that *ishto* is gonna sleep here too?" the Mono asked.

"Yeah," el Tripa answered without looking back.

El Cascara whispered, "At least today he already chose one."

"Yes, poor kid."

"Ah *púchica*, at least he's not gonna feel nothing."

The new little tenant looked at them oblivious of it all.

Chapter 6
Would You Think of Me?

The red wine worked through his system and, recognizing the same effects in his companion, he proposed the exploration of their bodies in the privacy of his room. They ran the few blocks from the bar where the seduction class had begun. Taking advantage of the tenuous light that illuminated the entrance like the glow of candles, he kissed her as one kisses a bottle of life. He swallowed her salty juice and a gush of desired dripped from their lips.

Bouncing off the walls, they descended to the basement of the old house on Washington Blvd. where he'd rented a room since he had left the nest. His parents loved him and hadn't wanted him to leave but they understood that leaving home was the American way to independence. A golden letter A adorned the wood door. The box, as the Ishto called his room, was on the verge of witnessing his last night with Wendy.

With a feline ability he lit the match and then the thick red candle he'd left on the nightstand. He tore off his shirt while she hurled away the black dress that had almost burst away from breasts displaying hard nipples that matched her lover's tool of passion. He kissed her neck then turned her around. He caressed her shoulders and kissed the scar on the undulation formed by the last vertebra. He kissed her *nalgas,* her buttocks, like one kisses a pillow before going to sleep. She loosened a moan suffocated in a whisper warning her about the lack of insulation. He'd discovered how easily sound traveled when his landlord called while he enjoyed a porno because the sounds disturbed the tenants on the first floor.

She broke free and disappeared into the bathroom. He, with his member mimicking a swing set, waited impatiently by the bed; he had always wondered what the hell women do in the bathroom moments before giving themselves to their man. He'd concluded that everything was a component of the erotic game, and that there were questions never meant to be asked. Women never asked men what they thought about when they were on the verge of breaking and stoically restrained the urgency to prolong the moment. Some thought about baseball, others counted to ten or twenty if that was necessary. He, he simply tightens his abdominal muscles and prays to the Creator to allow him more moments of life...

She returned. Her figure threw an equally beautiful shadow that danced on the wall, the floor, the ceiling. He stood up and, a little ashamed, wanted to cover the force that fought his boxer-briefs. She smiled and seemed pleased. Only a man knew how necessary that smile, half pleasing and half admiring, was to provide the confidence necessary for a man to feel...macho. He approached, and the extension of his body caressed her bellybutton. They kissed, caressed, and embraced. Then he knelt down with the confidence of knowing what she liked and, without lowering the red embroideries of her Victoria's Secret, buried his face in the vertex of desire.

Upon inhaling the bittersweet scent, he knew that she who would leave for Europe in less than twenty-four hours was the one. Waldo had said it was too soon to think that way. "And what do you know?" he had snapped perhaps to convince himself Waldo wasn't right; although he was. She pushed his face deeper and he felt the humidity of the maddening threshold. He lifted her up and carried her to the bed and got rid of what hindered. Her skin shone in the dancing light of the candle. He lay atop her and moved her blond hair to one side. She slid her hands beneath the cotton that covered his waist and played with the little hairs that adorned the fissure of his firm buttocks. Now he started moaning.

He went down on her pausing three times on the journey. First at her pink nipples that aimed towards Venus. He kissed them, he licked them, he gave them playful bites that made her forget her name. Then he continued his voyage. He stopped before her bellybutton where her piercing was the only bulk on the plain of her stomach. He penetrated with his tongue and tasted the cocoa flavor of her body lotion. He followed his path towards the door of the infinite and, once he found it, his tongue was the key and his desire the turning force. The scent reminded him of his favorite place: the beach. The rumble of waves and the sensual movement of the sea matched what was happening in his bed. He dominated her and he let her dominate him. With her smooth legs hooked over his shoulders, he watched her joy. With her legs around his hips, he watched her mount this man turned sexual animal. The candle was guttering and the sublime moment was approaching.

"Would you think of me when you get to Europe?" he asked grasping for air.
"Our connection is not about thinking. It's about feeling."
Their bodies were bathed in sweat and their muscles obliged the awaited spasm. She raised her hips and dropped them forcefully as her nails stabbed his shining shoulders and with that, she

assured him that she too had savored the ambrosia.

"When will you be back?" he asked.

"Soon. Don't worry. I'm taking some of you in me."

"It's too soon to think that way," Waldo had told him. Time and a text that read *I've found someone who understands me better. I don't wanna hurt you but don't wanna cheat on you either. I wanna be free to explore. Bye Ishto,* cuídate, *take care,* would prove him right. That night after dropping her off at her place, his dreams would be burned again.

Chapter 7
90 Milligrams of Reality

She is beautiful. With dark eyebrows sheltering eyes as black as jade stones: millenarian stone, sacred stone, beautiful rock that reflects in its interior the revolt and the solitude of its ancestors. Her white-as-goat-milk complexion was a gift from her father who also gave her memories of her mother, his wife, the woman who left without teaching her everything she needed to know and all he needed to improve. Her black-as-wild-jet hair was a gift from the one who no longer lived with them. Her graceful figure matched her dangerous *coquetería,* flirting. Her reflection in the mirror tells her she is beautiful and can get anything she wants in life because she's part of the generation of Latinas who've found the perfect amalgam of beauty and intelligence.

First in her class, first in the wet dreams of many young guys who never dared speak to her. First in everything she set her mind to but she would be the last one giving in to a man without having his heart first. After hearing the love story between his nomadic Cuban father and her mother, the one originally from Puebla, she decided to create a connection with her mother by having with her future husband a relation just like the one she once had with her father, the man who everyday feels more and more lonely. She wanted to discover the carnal love with him. She wanted to live with him what their parents lived. She wanted to vicariously live the life of her mother, which had been truncated by destiny. Her search had long been finished. If it were up to her, and if that someone were not so confused, she would already be taking grandkids to don Gustavo, her father.

Don Gustavo left Cuba when the embargo started. To this day he swears one could see him in the crowd in the airport scene in *Memories of Underdevelopment* heading towards the unknown. He left with a few rags in the suitcase, whatever they allowed him to carry in his pocket, and his psychiatrist diploma under his arm. He lived for almost six years in Miami but grew tired of exiled politicians who were impossible to cure with daily motivational chats or even by prescribing 90 milligrams of reality every day. The retired Anglo-Saxons of south Florida didn't seek his help because they were too superior to pay this Cuban whose accent made them feel like they were in an episode of the *I Love Lucy* show.

He had always thought that the problem of the American people was their lack of desire to rest even when they retire. The word retirement sounded like a conviction to retire from living. The word for retirement in Spanish was *jubilación,* which literally meant jubilation; that was intended because after they have worked hard all their lives, the individual deserve to relax or, as they said here, take it easy. Here they did not understand. So he decided to leave and his search for crazy people took him to Puebla, Mexico, a beautiful and pleasant place. While he was leaving the bus depot the thought "I will find my wife here" covered him but the blanket of optimism fell to the ground by a slap from the young lady in front of him with wild black hair like a *potra,* a stallion.

"*Descarado infeliz,* you shameless bastard", said the prettiest infuriated lady he had ever seen. "How dare you grope me?"
In the commotion the laughter of three kids rose from nearby. "*No señorita, el buen mozo no hizo nada.* No miss the stud didn't do anything,"

said one old lady with a face as withered as a raisin and whose voice escaped easily from a toothless mouth. "Those *escuintles,* kids, did it."

She pointed to the three friends who suddenly laughed no more. The young lady realized the Cuban could not be capable of such impertinence, not without having asked permission ahead of time that was. And she distributed blows to the three boys. Gustavo prepared to offer aid in case the kids retaliated. They were so confused by the *porrazos,* blows, they ran away.

The girl, now blushing red like a tomato, gathered her things from the floor. The old woman of the *perraje multicolor,* multicolor quilt, whispered to Gustavo, *"Pa' luego es tarde mozote, no se me agüite que de aquí en adelante, todo lo demás sabrá a puritita miel.* Don't get scared, stud. From now on everything will taste like pure honey," and pushed him down next to the *fierecilla,* the furious one. He smiled and helped her with her books. She apologized then they had *un agua fresca,* a drink.

Four years passed before they realized they were in love, three more before they married and another four until Teresita came into the world to seal the union of the Cuban with the *poblana.* For six years they enjoyed their little girl until Teresa left Gustavo sleeping with their memories and Teresita living alongside a profound emptiness. Two years after her death, he decided to undertake a second trip towards El Norte only this time he'd go further north. These were the Eighties, and many Latin Americans were migrating and surely they needed therapy in their own language to deal with the culture shock. Thus he imagined; the reality was different.

He made peace with that; he believed he would only be there a short time. Castro, his exiled friends assured him, would fall the following year so it was just a matter of time before he could reopen his clinic in Havana. Teresa had taught him to save for the future and to work hard so he was ready for anything. Plus, this time he was not alone. He would bring with him the fruit of their love, which gave him strength to fight.

Ten years later he practice at his house and was an advisor at Washington-Lee High School where Tere attended. Although the number of Latino students increased during that time, unfortunately the number who graduated did not. So, yes, life had once again smiled on him. At times, when the nostalgia embraced his thoughts and he'd drowned his memories in mojitos, he watched Tomás Gutiérrez Alea's film and would freeze the picture at the point where he left his beloved Cuba. At that particular moment the clock of his memory stopped to contemplate the injustice and never continued its endless march forward. He could still feel the weight of his body hitting the wet pavement before he stepped aboard. It had taken seconds but it had lasted a lifetime. Yes, he better than anyone else knew how someone's life could change in a split second.

Chapter 8
Their Luggage was Just a Pair of Backpacks Strapped Over Their Shoulders

It's Friday night, as always, they would go out. That night would be Adams Morgan in Northwest D.C. A great band, still underground, was playing a local club. Tere was on the VIP list of the best nightclubs in town so it was her job to come up with a plan every Friday. She found dates for everyone but somehow Ishto's never showed up or had to leave early so "destiny" determined Tere and Ishto would always finish the night together.

"If I depended on you to get laid, my rubbers would expire in my medicine cabinet, Tere!"

Ishto picked up la Tere and el Waldo before heading to his parent's home to get *la bendición,* their blessings, money they always gave him for the weekend. He really didn't need it because the three of them share expenses but he accepted the gift so as not to hurt their feelings.

The house smelled like jasmine. Janis loved burning incense and listening to Bob Dylan on Friday nights. He made her remember when young people still believed on the *power of the people* slogan. Ishto did backup whenever she sang *How does it feel?/ How does it feel?/ To be on your own, with no direction home/ Like a complete unknown/ Like a rolling stone*. It was their favorite song and the one that, according to her, reflected the feeling of any immigrant. They also share the vote on their favorite song from the other Janis, Janis Joplin.

This was not a conventional marriage. That had been their plan when they'd united lives back in the Seventies. Both had been attending the University of Berkeley at a time when being conventional was not permissible. Circumstances and desires called out for change; she as Bob embraced it and enjoyed it. After five years of living together, these couple of crazy lovers with the names of famous singers had visited nearly all of Latin America but they'd never gone to Guatemala. One evening after making love under a Peruvian poncho, they'd decided to visit the Land of the Mayans.

"You know it is dangerous out there?" Bob asked.

"You know it is dangerous up here, too," had been her answer.

"The government says that we shouldn't travel there."

"Don't worry, honey. There are plenty of American troops there."

Bob probably would have agreed to anything she'd asked. He still remembered how her eyes had become lost in a tunnel of confusion when they found the stork bleeding between her legs and her dream of motherhood drowned in a scarlet lake. Their tears washed the spot from the sheet but not the memory of the boy who was never delivered.

They arrived in Guatemala the last week of January 1980 to a country sunk in military repression and poverty. Despite that, Janis loved it immediately. She'd be eternally thankful for the country having given back what life had taken from her just months earlier. They boarded public transportation rather than the typical taxi to downtown. Their luggage was just a pair of backpacks strapped over their shoulders. That's the way they were: simple, sincere and easygoing. They were viewed with wonder by some passengers and distrust by others. But Janis would strike up a conversation with anyone.

"The *gringa* is friendly, no?" one woman commented when they got off the bus.

And somebody called, "Oh yeah, don't forget that our close friendship with the *gringos* began with Castillo Armas."

Nobody responded but everyone understood.

"Come on, you guys," Janis said, "sit with me. Oh, look at you Tere, so pretty."

The three took a seat in the living room. The red sofa was piled with multiple colorful cushions, worthy promotions of the Flower Generation. The two visitors were fascinated by Ishto's parents; although when the family was together, their physically differences came to the fore. Bob's and Janis' hair was as blond as corn silk, and they both had blue eyes. Ishto, legally Angel Durant according to his adoption papers, had black hair and eyes like coal.

Although physically very different, destiny had united them. When they were together, no one could doubt he was their son. "Bob is very good in the sack but I doubt he'd been able to make one as handsome as my Ishto," Janis would say with that freshness worth listening to. Tere and Waldo knew the Ishto had been adopted but he'd never discussed the circumstances. That night el Ishto would, for the very first time, share the flames burning his dreams.

Chapter 9
His Nightmare has Finally Become a Reality

By the time they arrived to the club, *el reventón,* the party, had already begun. Tere had once again hit the nail on the head, although it seemed the occupancy limit had been greatly ignored. Multicolor lights bathed the young people gathered on the dance floor as the opening band "Thoughts On Standby" played an original. Waldo went for the drinks.

He preferred hanging out at the bar because according to him it was the best way to lay the ground for later. He would play the gentleman card by capturing the bartender's attention whenever a beautiful girl wanted a drink. His rationale was that the second time they spotted each other she would be more comfortable with him. The technique worked most of the time but one girl's fiancé had not appreciated the gesture. Waldo ignored his presence and pressed on with trying to pick her up. The guy swung at him but before his fist landed, el Ishto was on his shoulders. Obviously they had called it a night.

This time Waldo never returned with the drinks. La Tere mingled with her date and el Ishto went to the men's room where he found some weed and as the song declared... he was no longer a real person just an illusion. He didn't smoke regularly but from time to time he'd take some hits. In these places it was so easy to find grass and pills. By the time he came out flying over the clouds, the place looked like a red line Metro train during rush hour. The main band had taken the stage. He stayed by the men's room; it was impossible to get near the stage.

The band played a tune and invited people to join in. The smoke machine filled the air. Mixed with the lights, it created a surreal atmosphere Ishto immediately disliked. Suddenly he was transported into his nightmare. A curtain on the side of the stage caught fire. The flames extended to the front of the stage. The crowd thought it was part of the show. But Ishto knew something was wrong.

When the flames reached the main guitarist from behind, he screamed. That sparked the hysteria. Pushes, shoves, shouts...the chaos had begun. Like the boy in his nightmare, Ishto curled up on the floor while everyone stepped on him. Mirrors and bottles burst as everyone ran towards an emergency exit blocked by the sound system. Waldo, who had seen everything from his hunting perch at the bar, rushed his companion outside and returned to look for Tere. He couldn't find her in the multitude; meanwhile the fire gained force. Suddenly somebody took hold of his leg.
"Where's Ishto?"
Panic lit her eyes. He picked her up and told her to leave. She wanted to hang onto him but the mob dragged her away like a stone at the mercy of a rampant river. Waldo dove in the mass and swam as his instinct guided him. He finally found Ishto as he had never seen him before. He was curled up on the floor palsied with fear. He was bathed in sweat and sucking his thumb like a child.
"Ishto, let's go, bro."
He did not move. His nightmare had finally become a reality. Waldo pushed him into the men's room and closed the door. The smoke

snaked under the door. He torn off his shirt, soaked it in water and covered his and Ishto's faces as he dragged him to the rear of the room. He embraced him as hard as he could. But the lack of consciousness made him see without seeing, feel without feeling. A shiver told him that this was the end; the end of his life and perhaps the end of his nightmare. That same nightmare he had tried so hard to forget. The explosions. The paintings melted by flames. Men with their faces covered by red bandanas, machetes waving. The boy he saw through the metal bars surrounded in flames begging for the truth.

First thick smoke...then tenuous smoke...later fine smoke...and then just thin smoke. Smoke escaping as sighs forgotten in some room blackened by a memory that disappeared in the cycles of time. The phone broke the vision. Tere shouted, *"¡Dónde estás!* Where are you? Did you find him? These motherfuckers don't let me back in."

"Cálmate, relax. He's alright and I think everything is OK now. I don't see smoke no more."

"The ambulance's here. Where are you?"

"In the men's room."

"Officer, my friends are in the men's room," she said to someone else. "They're going for you now."

"Cálmate, Tere, we're OK. How about you?"

"I'm OK but there are a bunch of people burnt and shit."

"Wait, here they come...it's over, Tere."

Chapter 10
I've Always Been Threaten by the Flames

"I know you kids and particularly Latinos don't believe in what we do but let me tell you that all these strange phobias and dreams, especially if they are repetitive, are not normal. I didn't want to intrude but since Teresita mentioned something I'd suggested to her that you come see me. No, don't get mad *chico,* kid, she didn't betray your trust. She cares about you and Waldo, another one who should come see me because of all that obsessive writing. Far from inspiration, it seems to me he has OCD. He's next. But let us focus on you *muchacho,* boy. Tell me how you feel."

El Ishto had been lost in thoughts that vanished when silence embraced the studio-cum-doctor's office. It was his turn to say something so he offered something simple.
"I wonder when El Buena Vista Social Club will play the Patriot Center?"
"Mira Ishto, if you don't feel comfortable talking to me, I can recommend someone else who can--"
"No, Doctor Gutiérrez, it's not you, it's me."
"Ah no, *chico,* that excuse might work with your *noviecitas,* your girlfriends, but you're going to do better with me because--"
"That's not what I meant. What happens is that, I don't even know where to begin."
"*Bueno chico,* just start from the beginning. *Vamos,* let's go."
"Well...look, the problem is that I don't even know when this whole thing started. I mean, since I can remember I've always been threaten by flames and everything that has to do with fire.

Once, I don't know if Tere told you, I made a scene at a restaurant when a waiter brought a dish with some type of meat, you know, surrounded by flames." He was terribly embarrassed.

"And what about the *sueños,* the dreams?"

"*Sueños? Jah,* those are nightmares and they're always the same."

"*A ver, a ver,* let's see, what do you mean the same?"

"It always happens in a room in the second floor of a house. Well, I think it's the second floor 'cuz I can see the sky and the leaves of trees through windows covered with metal bars. I think it's an office...yeah, it's got to be an office 'cuz it has official photos and it's very professional looking, you know what I mean? The room has velvet curtains, which gives it a European look. There are paintings but it's difficult to see their theme 'cuz they're smothered by flames. I can't breathe. The rough smoke scrapes my throat. Everyone steps on me trying to save themselves."

"Then there are other people there."

"Oh, yeah. The smoke doesn't let me distinguish anyone in particular. But there are people *amontonados,* gathered, by the window and some are on the other side. The window glass explodes; there's infernal heat."

While describing the scene, he started to sweat and found breathing difficult. He had closed his eyes, and in spite of the pain he wanted to relive the experience. This dream had been part of his life for so long he needed to know why it haunted him. Doctor Gutiérrez wrote everything in his notebook then asked, "Do these faces look familiar? Do you recognize anyone?"

"I don't see faces. Actually the dream always ends when I look out the window like I'm looking for something or somebody."

"Do you think you've been there before?"

"No. Never. Although I kinda feel very familiar with that place. But it must be 'cuz I've been dreaming it since I can remember."

Don Gustavo noticed that Ishto's eyes were still closed. "Are you still in the room?"

"No, I don't see anything no more."

"*Muy bien*, very well, open your eyes and take a sip of water."

El Ishto found himself soaked in sweat.

"*No te preocupes,* don't worry. You're traumatized and it's normal for you to react this way. It would be worse if your mind pretended that everything is well and tried to hide this tragic episode in your life in self-defense."

"But you don't understand. This is not something I lived. It's just a dream, that's all."

"Would it bother you if I speak with your parents?"

Chapter 11
Hunting Muses

He enjoyed the humid nights of summer in the metropolitan area; the humidity that washed his body and rinsed his face. In winter, the cold pecked his forehead and burned his skin until it changed the color of his face, turning it into a leaf lost in a season that did not belong to him. He embraced all the sensations that allowed him to feel alive. It was strange that someone from a hot climate could enjoy two such opposite seasons. Perhaps life would be more bearable if we accepted it as it comes, he thought. Perhaps we'd be happier if we allowed our feeling to take charge. Living life simply without so many existential anguishes. Without worrying about finding the answers to all the whys. If it came to us to cry, just cry; if we were to laugh, just laugh. Living every moment one hundred percent.

Waldo couldn't live life that way. Waldo, with his little pocketbook stuck to his ribs, looked for the answers to the whys and would not stop until he found them. At the very least he would write about his search. That search and his desire to write had both become obsessions. Once he forgot his pocketbook and was so desperate to record his notes he'd arrived home with his forearms covered with scribbles that had been impossible to decipher. To this day he swore those had been his best phrases yet and that he would never recall them again.

He decided to take a walk and think about the best way to help his friend. What was happening to el Ishto was not only rare but also intriguing. It couldn't be possible that a simple dream would affect a human so much, could it?

Not a simple dream. Then he heard André Bretón, *Automatisme psychique pur par lequel on se propose d'exprimer, soit verbalement, soit par écrit, soit de toute autre manière, le fonctionnement réel de la pensée en l'absence de tout contrôle exercé par la raison, en dehors de toute préoccupation esthétique ou morale...* to use dreams to solve the problems of life.

With that thought stirring his subconscious, he walked until the streetlights grew tenuous and the shadows deepened. He had ventured to a dirty, smelly, trash-strewn place. The streetlights revealed houses stained by graffiti. Fear itched his back and curiosity immediately scratched it. So he continued walking towards a story he might tell, hunting muses. The snores of a couple of homeless people resting on newspapers updating the number of casualties from a war that had started based on a faulty intelligence report echoed around him. He stepped on the ruins of a beer bottle with the remains of a yellowish liquid swishing inside. A woman wearing a tight dress scraped the sidewalk with her high heels.

She approached him and asked, *"¿Qué buscas, papi?* What are you looking for, sweetie? I give you what you want. Mine's still *apreta'ito,* tight, and if you're looking for *pinga,* dick, I have a wonderful strap-on that will make you scream."

He smiled and continued walking.

"C'mon, *papi,* don't go! Can't you see that business is a bitch tonight?"

He walked a little bit faster. She stayed behind begging for the coin of life. After another few blocks, he stopped in front of a house whose beautiful facade had been disfigured by the blows of time. After hiding himself in the dark so as not to contaminate the scene with his presence, he observed the human trade. He recorded in his little notebook everything he saw, and even what he didn't.

That night when he returned home and ran tripping up the stairs, not even the *"Puta* Waldo, we're trying to sleep!"* coming from his parents' room stopped him. The next morning he woke surrounded by a few wrinkled pieces of paper telling the story of *La Niña, The Young Girl* who had been born bathed by the glow of the streetlight that slid by his window.

Chapter 12
La Niña, The Young Girl

It's 9:40 p.m. and the girl––still a child really––is about to leave her apartment on Columbia Road. While her two little brothers live the reality found in dreams, her mom does the same with her constant companion, a bottle of liquor. The Math homework will have to wait because solving fractions loses its value when raised to the fifth power of reality.

While she sprays herself with cheap perfume and applies the heavy makeup that masks her tender youth, her soul abandons her body. Only this way can she allow herself be touched by those who pay a pittance for the services of one who should be planning her sweet sixteen party. Instead she bears the weight of repulsive old men whose cologne a mix of sweat and alcohol night after night put their manhood to the test with her without ever realizing that it's precisely their manhood that is lost between their moans and groans.

The sweater, two sizes too big, covers the skintight dress that attracts any number of customers young and old. In a black plastic bag she carries the high heels that make her look taller, and in her purse she holds the keys to the apartment so she won't lose them like she long ago lost the keys to happiness. The mantle of darkness helps her lose herself on the Avenue of Oblivion where she starts her journey towards perdition, towards consecration, towards those green American dollars that will bring food to the ones now drifting off into dreams of flying away with Harry Potter.

She arrives at the usual corner and greets her colleagues with a smile. Then she lives the uncertainty of anxious waiting. There, under the streetlight that illuminates the evening's merchandise, she wonders whether her future would have been different had he––the one in the torn picture, the one without a face, the one without a name, the one who got caught by *La Migra*, the Immigration Department––not left her with the woman who calls herself her mom but whose actions cast that into doubt. Maybe she would continue being poor but at least she wouldn't have to open herself to anyone. Nor would she have to exchange her teenage years for those of an adult, nor would she have to rush headlong into the future not realizing that it is best for her to take things slow...

And slowly, very slowly, a station wagon pulls over across the street. It's time to get to work, she tells herself. The driver gestures to call her over. She thinks he's calling her over. Her legs tremble but she walks towards the car... "I missed you *papi,* daddy," says a young guy who runs from behind her. He leans on the driver's side of the car. She watches as a fat, hairy hand emerges from the window and grabs the guy's ass as if checking the merchandise. They talk briefly, the advantage of regular customers. He hurries around to the passenger's side. Mike will go home early tonight, she thinks as she feels a touch of envy. But tomorrow she'll learn that Mike never returned home.

One by one the fireflies of the night extinguish their light and fly away. One by one kids her age enter and exit cars old and new while she keeps on waiting, always waiting. Waiting for someone to take her away and pay her for a moment of pleasure. Waiting for someone to pay her for letting him smell her, feel her, touch her, and sometimes even hurt her. Waiting for her existence to change. She wonders how different it would be if she were dead but this feeling evaporates as soon as she sees her little brothers, who remind her of her purpose in life. She smiles at the sight of them enjoying their food even as she carries the burden of knowing their food was bought with money she got while performing the business of carnal desire.

Finally a car stops in front of her. In her desperation, she thanks God. The negotiation happens quickly because the man is horny and ready to come. He drives two blocks. She looks at the face reflected in the passenger's mirror and barely recognizes her own features. He turns down a dark alley, the gift of one of the several *maras* that rule this section of the city. She starts working. Her inexperienced mouth goes up and down without stopping to hear her client's foul words. She weighs a few ounces less; her soul, which has finally abandoned her, is suspended in front of the car observing. Her body, without soul or essence, has become a well-oiled machine that does its job...up and down...up and down...up and down. She feels the tension in his fat, hairy thighs and she hurries so she can return to the corner to continue working and she wonders if she'll ever feel pleasure doing this...No, a little voice whispers and is silenced by the "Yeah, yeah!" of her satisfied client.

The dollars earned are secured in a bra that hugs her pubescent breasts. Afterwards this little girl returns to the corner where she started. Tonight she'll have to return there twice more because the rent is due at the end of the week. The thought of her little brothers helps to insulate her soul from putrid reality.

On her way back home, she thinks about what she was, what she is, and what she will be. Once again her little brothers' smiles remind her she's doing what her life requires. The one who watches from above knows that even when she soils her body with her customers' sweat and even when her hands are stained cleaning up her mom's vomit, she remains pure. That watcher sends her a shooting star. She sees it, closes her eyes and makes a wish....

Chapter 13
The Documentary Began

"We wanted to come see you but thought we should call first," Tere said. She was on speaker so Waldo could jump in.

"Come on, you guys!" Ishto said. "You know you don't need to call first."

"We know but *no queríamos molestar,* we didn't wanna bother, you know."

"We? You mean you, Waldo said. "Me and Ishto are like bothers. Am I right or not, Ishto?"

"Yeah, sure. Whatever you say, man. But seriously guys, I'm OK now. Plus, I think talking to your dad, Tere, really helped. By the way, I saw some genuine Cubans cigars there so tell him if he ever tells anyone what we talked about in the session, I'll call his compatriots in *la Pequeña Habana* down in Florida."

"Ay, Ishto, not even when you're sick! You let that alone."

"*¡Señores Imperialistas no les tenemos ningún miedo!*" Waldo shouted. "Imperialistic gentlemen, we are not afraid of you!"

"C'mon, Waldo. You and your quotes, man! That's an easy one." Ishto guessed most of Waldo's quotes when he tested his knowledge.

"That's a phrase painted on a wall in Havana," Tere said cutting the game short. "Anyways, we called to see if you wanna to go to the preproduction meeting with those students. You know, the ones who wanna us to shoot some B-roll while they gather in front of the Capitol to manifest against... something, I'm not sure... next week. The meeting is in a church by Capitol Hill."

"Gosh, and why so religious all of a sudden?"

"Yeah, I know.... Well, what happens is that they're gonna attend a talk with some Guatemalan relatives of *desaparecidos,* missing persons, you know, during the civil war. I'm pretty sure you know everything about that terrible war."

In reality Ishto knew little; he had never been interested in the subject.

"It seems that these guys are deep into this whole deal about human rights and mass organization."

"Oh, then I think el Ishto should definitely go," Waldo said. "See if they can help him organize his encephalic mass."

Ishto knew Tere had pinched his arm when Waldo yelped.

"Don't worry guys, I'll go," Ishto said. "I can't just stay in my room all day. Besides, now that Wendy...." He hadn't yet told them about her text message.

"Well, she's not here...."

Tere made an annoyed sound when she heard that name.

"I need to go out and...just go out, you know," Istho said.

"Good. We'll talk later, then. I'm taking this one home. He claims he's gonna start working on the script for the commercial we're shooting next week and I'm gonna see this *doña,* miss, to see if I can convince her that a kickass TV commercial produced by us would increase her sales."

"Cool. Good luck with that."

"Perhaps we can do something tonight?"

"Sure."

They said their goodbyes. By the time he arrived, the presentation had already begun. A large screen had been set up in front of the altar and a projector connected to a DVD player on standby awaited the commanding index finger. He hadn't visited a church for some time. It had been a while since he'd last heard the echoes fluttering off walls that had once been immaculately white but now wore a gray mantle dyed by candles, each a sacred offering blazing out in hopes of a miracle.

For a moment his memory offered the scent of flowers and burning candles. His footsteps waded into the thin layer of tears washing the floor and for a moment he was transported to another place...different but similar. Bathed in incense and taken by his right hand by an old woman. He never saw her face but he remembered that hand cut by hard work and time as well as its warmth and security. Together they had walked up the stones tumbled at the entrance of a church lost in memory.

The old woman wore a *corte* and a *guipil* like the one the middle-age woman seating at the front table wore. A man seated beside her wore the male version of the traditional clothes. They were near the screen, and to their left were people who appeared to be the event organizers. The church wasn't full but sufficient liberals were in attendance to satisfy the optimists.

Next to the Guatemalan couple, separated by another person, was a woman of brilliant black hair and wide-awake glance. Her presence attracted Ishto immediately. He almost forgot the couple from the northern region of Guatemala. For a moment, for just a moment, the world contained just her and him and nobody else. She was Doctor Scarlet, he discovered during the presentation. She taught in none other than his Alma Matter, specifically in the School of International Studies. That semester she was teaching Political Violence in the Americas.

Funny how he'd never seen her on campus, much less heard of her. Was she a new faculty member? She must have not been teaching long; she looked mature but not old. After the formal introductions the doctor, so young, so attractive, so sensual, stood. Her gestures were so delicate, her figure was fit, and she had a panther's agility that drew his eyes like a magnet. From her lips he learned she'd been teaching for some time and constantly took sabbaticals to lead an investigation, to attend conferences, or to write books. So writing was one of her passions... he wondered about the others.

She had traveled to almost all the Latin America countries. *"Amo su cultura,* I love its culture," she said, and he'd never felt so eager to tell someone he was from Guatemala. Her silver silk blouse invited the imagination and her tight leather pants proved she was an unconventional professor. Glasses with black hoops adorned her eyes, a perfect amalgam of knowledge and playfulness.

Today's chat dealt with the disappearances of Guatemalan natives carried out by a brutal government. El Ishto thought the guerrillas must share some responsibility too. He couldn't believe the government was the only bad character in this film. He sure would have the opportunity to ask the doctor. During her presentation, the people seated at the table were pointed out as survivors. On the table sat books like *I Rigoberta Menchú: An Indian Woman in Guatemala, The Battle for Guatemala, The New Politics of Survivor,* and *Bridges of Courage.* The right side of the table was empty. Doctor Scarlet gave the signal, the lights went out, and the documentary began.

Chapter 14
Si vivos se los llevaron...
If You Took Them Away Alive...

"SI VIVOS SE LOS LLEVARON..."

OPENING

FADE IN:

EXT. NATIONAL PALACE GUATEMALA CITY
The camera captures a peaceful march
of survivors and family members
carrying oversized pictures of
Desaparecidos (Disappeared). As they
pass by, prayers can be heard as:

Narrator (VO)
    More than 200,000 people died
    during the Guatemalan Civil War.
    Many families were destroyed in
    a period when massacres and
    torture became *"el pan nuestro
    de cada da"* (everyday business).
    Many had to bury loved ones
    without knowing why they had
    been killed. They achieved
    closure. But what about those
    who didn't have the chance to
    say goodbye? What about those
    who seek the truth? What about
    those who need to know? Today
    they gather at the National
    Palace to demand that...

CUT TO:
MAIN TITLE -

Marchers start to chant *"Si vivos se los llevaron...vivos los queremos"* (If you took them away alive...we want them back alive). The title appears as they repeat the phrase three times until it becomes just an echo. The title fades out along with audio.

The TITLE:

"SI VIVOS SE LOS LLEVARON...VIVOS LOS QUEREMOS"

FADE OUT

SCENE ONE

FADE IN:

INT. LAURA'S DINING ROOM

LAURA
"Aquí estábamos comiendo cuando unos hombres entraron y a punta de pistola se lo llevaron. A mi hijo Jacinto le metieron un culatazo en la mollera que por poco me lo matan. Y ya nunca volví a saber de mi Chepe." (Translation subtitled in yellow text) -We were right here just eating when a group of armed men came in and took him. They hit my son Jacinto in the head. It almost killed him. And I never saw my poor *Chepe* again.

FADE OUT

END OF SCENE ONE

SCENE TWO

FADE IN:

EXT. DOÑA JUANA'S HOME

DOÑA JUANA
"*Aquí estaba yo parada cuando vi a los judiciales montarlo al jeep. Allí nomás dejó tirados sus libros. Era bien educado, siempre me saludaba antes de irse a estudiar. Yo mejor me entré. Qué podía yo hacer toda vieja y bruta. Le hice un tesito de tilo a la mamá, doña Chucita y se lo llevé.*"
(Translation subtitled in yellow text) - I was standing right here when the military put him in the jeep. He left his books right there on the sidewalk. He was well-mannered, he always said hi to me when he left home to go to school. When I saw what happened, I went inside my home. Besides, what could I have done? I am old. I did make a cup of tea for his mom; *doña* Chucita and I took it to her.

NARRATOR (VO)
These are just a few examples of
what Guatemalans have suffered
throughout the war, a war that
has destroyed many...

Chapter 15
They Both Flirt Shamelessly

"So you're a doctor, ah?" Ishto asked.

"That's right...what? What is it? Is it that perhaps I don't own the authoritative voice?"

He smiled. "Well, let's just say that the doctors I've known don't look like you. Although I must confess that with you I feel comfortable saying aaaah." He opened his mouth wide.

"Oh, I see you're the *chistoso,* the class clown."

"Not *el chistoso,* doctor. Simply the one who entertains the group when the lessons get boring."

"I see. In my years of teaching I've encountered a few. So, *¿cómo te llamas?*"

She meant to ask his name but el Ishto played with its meaning by answering the other meaning of the question.

"I don't call myself. People call me, and I must say that when I'm lucky, they call me pretty often."

"So you know Spanish enough to play with semantics."

Her soft accent when she spoke Spanish massaged his neck and relaxed his muscles. El Ishto smiled. For some reason they both flirted shamelessly. And perhaps I'm mistaken but I could swear the doctor was also leaving aside her profession, the age difference and everything else to accept her own essence, that of a sensual and attractive woman.

"So how am I going to call you if you don't give me your name?"

"Well, Doctor, you can--"

"Doctor? I believe we left formality behind when you first showed me the cavities in your molar."

"Those damn chocolates. You know, Doctor...sorry, Kathy."

"I wouldn't have guessed you too were a victim of chocolates." She looked his body over.

"I have a high metabolism. It seems like I'm always accelerated."

"Yes, I noticed that you move fast."

"But I also know how to slow down."

"Good. So slow down for a minute and tell me your name."

"My friends call me Ishto." He looked directly into her eyes but couldn't stare for too long. His gaze dropped to the paper plate he held with a couple of *tostadas de salsa* that had been perfectly deep-fried.

"Ishto? Isn't that what Guatemalans call a child? I lived in Guate for a little while but if I remember correctly they also use *patojo*. So you are...."

"Yes, I was born there. But my parents are Americans."

"Well, if they were born on this continent, of course they are Americans, all of us born on the American continent are Americans. America goes from the Straits of Behring to Tierra de Fuego."

"Good Lord, another liberal," he whispered.

"What?"

"I'm sorry. I meant to say they are North Americans."

"They were living in Guate when they had you?"

"No, I am adopted."

"And...." She vacillated, and he intuited what her inquisitive mind wanted to know next.

"I never knew them," he said. "My adoptive parents found me or rather I found them on a bus heading for la Antigua."

She looked intrigued but decided not to dig any deeper. "Oh, la Antigua, what a beautiful city!"

"I couldn't tell. I don't remember it. In fact, I don't remember anything about my life in Guatemala."

"I do. As a matter of fact, I remember a lot. I miss *las tostadas con salsa.* Don't get me wrong, these are good but they pale in comparison. And what about the *atol de elote,* hot drink made of sweet corn, sold by the San Miguel church? I'm hoping to go back soon so I can finish my investigation. If you're interested, I can tell you more about Guate any time you want."

What irony. The *gringa* teaching a *chapín* about Guate.

"*Bueno,* Ishto, and what brings you here?" she asked. "Or is that perhaps you're finally interested in the subjects concerning your country of origin."

He looked for a ring on her left hand but the plate covered it. He wished he were Superman and had x-ray vision. "No, as a matter of fact, I was supposed to meet future clients here."

"Clients?"

"My friends and I have a company. We make TV commercial. DeLos Reyes Productions", he announced solemnly. Then he threw her a wink with a bold smile. "We shoot all kinds of videos."

She enjoyed the moment.

"So anyway," he said, "they wanted us to shoot them during a walk or something next week. But I don't see them."

"So that's your profession?"

"Yes, and believe it or not, I go to AU."

"No way! Well, I imagine you've taken the easy courses because I've never seen you in any of mine."

"I don't like the easy ones." He stared at her beautiful dark brown eyes. "I love challenges."

"I can assure you mine will be worth the effort."

"We're still talking about classes, right?"

"Of course, Ishto, of course."

They laughed like old friends. That afternoon, they chewed up the age difference and washed it down with Coke. They left the place almost touching each other's hands...and there was no ring.

Chapter 16
Good Weed

As soon as the door opened smoke from the incense fogged his glasses. They're smoking some good weed here, *chico*, don Gustavo thought, and with a warm smile he accepted the invitation to come in. He passed through a multicolor curtain made of breads and sat on an old but quite comfortable sofa in the living room. The scene recalled the Sixties, and the sound of music flying through the clouds helped him remember.

"What's up, Doc? We're so glad you came to visit us." Bob carried a red wine glass in each hand and offered one.

"We love Tere." Janis wore a very loose blouse beaded at the neck and arms that could have been a dress with a pair of faded jeans.

"Yes, I know. I feel the same about el Ishto, and that's why I wanted to talk to you about his nightmares."

"Yes, the nightmares," Bob said. "We remember them. Janis often had to climb into his bed until he'd fall back asleep. We treated him with all kinds of alternative methods but nothing worked. Then we tried our luck with the traditional ones, you know, taking him to the doctor and all those things but he never wanted to continue the visits. And as you know, when forced, not even sex is good."

"You mean food."

"Oh, I'm sorry, I'm the worst when it comes to sayings. But anyway, the idea is the same; humans need both. Honestly, I would say one more than the other." He threw a malicious glance at Janis.

"Bob," he said, "I believe we can discuss the psychology of sex some other time. Right now what worries me is your son."

"Yes, of course, but please, don Gustavo, tell us how we can help."

"Well, for starters, has he ever been in a fire?"

"No. Never. Well...just last week's but you already know about that one."

"And what about before you found him?"

"Well, Doc, we really don't know a lot about his past. He'd been probably six or seven years old when he found us on that bus. He doesn't have any scar, does he, Janis?"

"No. When he was small I used to give him baths but I never saw anything."

"In what circumstances did you find him?"

"Well," Janis said, "he pushed his way through the crowd and that was exactly how we finally got on as well. You know how it is in Latin America. *A mí me encantaba,* I loved it."

Bob got up and began singing *La Guagua* of Celia Cruz. *"Al fijarse que la guagua/ya viene por la rotonda/sale arrollando la gente/ como si fuera en la conga...."*

Janis joined him and they started to dance. Gustavo watched with disbelief but admired the grace these *gringos* demonstrated dancing to a Latin tune. He, a true Cuban, inconspicuously struck the floor with his heel. *"Para subir a la puerta/ se empujan unos a otros/ y a veces sufre la guagua/ desfiguración de rostro...."*

Then he remembered that this was a work meeting and as Bob yelled, *"Azucaaaa!"* Gustavo shouted, *"Señores, por favor esto es serio!* People, please, this is a serious matter!"

They both stopped dancing and somehow embarrassed, took their seats. "Sorry, Doc, but the smile is the best way to eliminate stress."

"Look, I don't know if it's stress or *los tres,* the three drinks, that already went to your head but we must behave like adults. Otherwise the boy is not going to get well."

"I'm sorry, don Gustavo. You're right but as we already told you, we don't know much."

"He was frightened," Janis said, "but he hadn't come from any fire. He was dirty but not burnt. When he found me in the seat, he threw himself at me like a shipwreck survivor who finds land. Of course I couldn't do anything other than hold him to my chest, and he immediately felt asleep."

"When he finally woke up, we were already in la Antigua. Later he said he lived with his friends in a landfill. He told us he'd climbed into a truck to flee the military and he'd ended up in the capital but he didn't know the village where he was from."

"Back then our Spanish wasn't very good and neither was his so we didn't understand each other very well. La Antigua was our first stop visiting Guatemala's countryside and by the time we came back to the city a couple of weeks later, we kinda loved him and I think he kinda loved us too. So we gathered all our savings and paid *la mordida,* the bribe, to get him out of the country. We figured his family had been assassinated by the damn army or the fucking Right. You know how things were back then."

"Sure but let us not forget that the fucking Left did some things, too," don Gustavo said.

"So that's everything we know, Doc," Bob said.

"Well, what we do in these cases is track back through history to find the origin of the problem," he said. "It's called regressive hypnosis."

"What?"

"Regressive hypnosis."

"Is it safe?"

"As you know, the mind is difficult to predict. Plus we need to find out if he doesn't have hipnofobia. If he agrees to the procedure, and I believe he will simply because I get the sense he is ready to take this pyrophobia on, I will be glad to offer my services."

"Well, if you think that'll help, we put him in your hands, Doc. We've known you for years and you're smart and very knowledgeable in spite of your political position."

Don Gustavo chose to ignore the comment but he did appreciate the recognition and even the honesty. "Where should we perform the session?"

"I think here'll be perfect," Bob said.

"Yes. You have maintained a surrealist atmosphere in here but nevertheless, I believe we must leave that decision to el Ishto."

"Good then," Janis said. "I'm so glad Tere was able to convince Ishto to come see you. She really is a great young woman in spite of--"

"In spite of what?" Don Gustavo was exasperated.

"No, Gus what we tried to--"

"Gustavo, please." The psychologist was about to cross the limits of his patience.

"Gustavo, what we meant to say is that we admire Tere and we respect her home and we are thankful that you respect ours."

"Good. What really matters here is el Ishto. I'll talk to him and will contact you both soon. I need to get going. And *coño,* please open the windows! I am beginning to see *babosadas,* hallucinations!"

Chapter 17
It's You, Ishto! It's You!

By the time only a squirt of Riesling sailed seductively around the base of the bottle, Ishto knew plenty about the doctor and she continued inventing theories about him. The remains of the spring rolls had cooled beneath the waning crescent moon that every so often was covered with a graceful veil of clouds.

She'd told him about her adventures in Chile protesting against Pinochet, in Nicaragua against Somoza, and El Salvador against her own government. He remained quiet. She'd laid out the thesis of her most recent book about the movements of pacific resistance in Latin America, and he'd still remained quiet. She'd felt old...but with a simple smile, seeing the ageless woman, he rekindled her desire to continue chatting and the monologue continued a few more hours.

They learned a lot about each other. He by listening, and she by watching his reactions to her views. Kathy'd been professor for a long time, so she knew how to differentiate those pretending not to listen from those traveling other places while pretending to listen. El Ishto belonged to the former.

"When did your parents bring you here?" Kathy asked.
"In 1980."
"Interesting. I was in Guatemala in 1980. I'd only planned to go for a week but after the tragedy I stayed longer."
"Did something happen to you?"
"No. I'm talking about the Spaniard Embassy massacre. Do you know about that?"

"No, not really."

"Well, in 1980 a group of *campesinos,* peasants, members of the *Comité de Unidad Campesina,* the Peasants Committee United, took the Spaniard Embassy. They wanted to force the Lucas García administration to listen to their demands. You know, something that was common in the eighties during government repression."

"Their action backfired though. The government refused to talk to them and instead of trying to bring the whole situation under control with a rational approach, you know, through negotiation, like the Spaniard ambassador trapped inside supplicated, security forces invaded the embassy. It was horrible! More than thirty people died, including two former Guatemalan dignitaries."

"How'd they die?"

"A fire broke out on the second floor where the *manifestantes,* protesters, took the hostages after the government broke the international law regarding embassy inviolability and entered by force. Vicente Menchú died there."

"Who?"

"Vicente Menchú, father of Rigoberta Menchú. The Nobel Peace Prize Winner."

"Sorry...don't follow the news."

She was disappointed.

"But did everyone die?" Ishto asked.

"Not everyone. The ambassador escaped and one of the *manifestantes* survived the fire."

"So they've talked...right?"

"Well, the *manifestante* disappeared. Well, they made him disappear. He was taken from the hospital. Later his body reappeared. He had been shot execution style in la San Carlos, you know the public University of San Carlos. A note on the body threatened the ambassador."

"What we know are the few details the ambassador shared. As you can imagine, the government and its followers tried to discredit him. They accused him of being an accomplice, which he's always emphatically denied, so hopefully with time we'll know more. But who knows…as you can see, I'm very much interested in this subject. If you want to know more, I've books that go deep in the subject."

"Can you imagine Ishto, being burned alive? Feeling the flames approach and not being able to escape? Feeling your breathing being suffocated by the heat and that…"

He couldn't hide his anxiety. In his nervousness, he fumbled with his glass and spilled the wine. He got up and walked to the window. Clouds flew by until one cluster covered the moon. The image covered Ishto with black smoke. He felt the heat again. He heard frightened shouts and felt his throat burn while breathing the acid that flooded the room. His eyes spilled blood.

The flames raged through the room. Paintings of beautiful women, their arms raised and their bodies adorned with fitted costumes with long trains of white veils, hung on the walls. The fandango dance here, the bullfight there. Everything surrounded in flames of yellow, white, blue and red, and on the ground the cowering boy in worn-out blue jeans and a *camisa a cuadros,* a checkered shirt.

Metal bars on the windows prevented escape. Furniture blocking the axe-torn wooden door burnt. Four people covered their faces with bandanas…were they protecting the entrance or guarding the exit? The boy shouted. The boy cried. Who was that boy? Who was that boy!

"It's you, Ishto! It's you!"

"No!" he shouted. "It's not me! *Déjame en paz,* leave me alone!"

And he slapped the pale blue napkin from Kathy's hand.

"Yes, *mírate,* look at you, you are the one bleeding. You must've stepped on the broken wine glass. Are you alright?"

"What?" he whispered.

She led him back to the sofa. Silently she tended his wound. He just sat there watching the smoke billow over his memory. That was not the first time she'd had to care for somebody wounded either physically or psychologically. In Chile she had cared for many *compañeros,* camrades who'd been tortured by the dictator's regime.

When she was done, they huddled together beneath a Mexican poncho. The monologue continued but this time, Ishto spoke. He talked about his phobia. He told her about his fear of the flames that incinerated his dreams. This time it was he who requested help. His eyes floated in tears.

They kissed, sharing the remains of the wine on their tongues. They embraced. He licked the remains of her perfume from behind her ears. She gently opened his shirt, pausing now and then while his fingertips caressed her rigid and rebellious nipples. She knelt in front of him and, while kissing his flat stomach, she eased open his belt buckle. The buttons of his jeans fought to contain the one trying to escape.

When she finally released him, he immediately sought the humid and thirsty lips of his *emancipadora,* his liberator, who kissed him without reserve and grasped him as a diver clings to an oxygen valve. While her pitch-black hair rushed like waves along the coastline of his hairless legs, he enjoyed the sublime rhythm. When he was on the verge of breaking, he stood and displayed the ship's mast ready to power the sailboat out to sea.

He guided her to the place where he had sailed the seven seas then unfolded his beautiful lady's mainsails. He slid past the undulations of her naked body and arrived at the natural well formed by the rocks of her thighs. He dove in, eager to swim until time infinite. Again and again he heard the song of a mermaid; again and again she sank her nails like gold anchors into his back.

Once he had satisfied his erotic thirst, he navigated up her shoreline stopping at the two islands. He continued up to her neck, leaving traces of her flavor imprinted at the site of each kiss. The escaped prisoner wanted to enter the humid cave surrounded by thick moss. With expert ability he sheathed the diver in a scuba suit and sent him on the expedition.

The young explorer found all kinds of precious stones: rubies, emeralds, sapphires, and jade submerged in sticky seaweed. He journeyed in and out, and on each trip he found something new. Finally he reached the bottom and found the desired pearl, the beautiful mermaid's heart... the Gem Spot. Instead of taking it, he struck it time and again until the moaning let him know it was time to surface. He struck four deep blows and together they spilled the juice of shared desire as the sun rose. Splashed by the breeze, they lay down on the sailboat and slept; she completely satisfied, and he certain that this time, at least this time, the flames would not burn his dreams.

Chapter 18
The Text Message

The text message from Tere was direct: *Ishto my dad wants to C U tomorrow @ your parent's... say around 4. He says he found a way to help you. Call me :)*

Chapter 19
10ª calle 6-20

"You must tell me everything you see... everything. Now take a deep breath and as you let it out, close your eyes and begin to feel yourself relaxing. That's right, good, you're doing fine.... As the seconds continue their infinite march, you begin to fall in a dream that becomes deeper and deeper and deeper...."

With a strong blow Hypnos flew him to another dimension. Ishto listened to the breathing of two bodies by his side. The three provided each other with warmth. The feeling of these bodies was new, yet familiar. The scent of waste sickened him but that too was familiar. When he finally found the will to open his eyes, he found two children thrown on a *petate* next to him.

"At the end of the room I see an immense bulk half covered by a dirty, frayed bed sheet. A hairy and obese arm comes out of it. The arm ends with a gigantic hand resting on a tiny bulk. The weight of this body is too great for the camp bed and almost touches the earth floor. The hairy hand goes under the sheets and begins to touch *el bultito,* the tiny bulk. The big bulk touches it first slowly, and soon with anxiety. Now the great mass rubs itself against the tiny one. I stared at it from *el petate.* The mountain of hair tries to get on top."

"Then it turns. He sees me with those blood-stained pupils. His rage paralyzes me. '*Qué putas mirás,* what the fuck are you looking at? You ishto, piece of shit.' The three of us stare and can't move. He gets up. His dirty worn-out underwear barely covers the arrow aimed at us. The small bulk is a boy just like me. I wanna make sure but I don't get to see no more 'cuz the hairy hand grabs me by the hair and sends me flying to the other side of the *champa,* the hut. My back hits the cardboard walls while my face scrapes against mud and stones. The whole *champa* vibrates."

"Kicks fall on the other two like a storm. 'Go to work, you lazy bastards! The newspapers are not gonna sell themselves, *cerotes.*' He crouches, throws the newspapers at us. His stained underwear is full of holes. His entire body is covered with hair. 'Get out!' We get dressed, take the newspapers and run out. As I wipe my bloody nose with the sleeve of my *camisa a cuadros,* I turn around. Through the torn curtain I see the beast balance itself time and time again on the *bultito. 'Apuráte vos,* hurry up!' the other boy says. 'What you are waiting for? *Otra vergueada?* Another beating?'"

Waldo, seated next to don Gustavo, writes everything in his notebook but nothing helps him understand the macabre scene. Don Gustavo continues the hypnosis therapy while thinking, *I'm going to have to talk to Janis and Bob again. We must be missing something.*

Kathy, sitting next to Janis, watches with anguish. Bob, who is next to Tere, exhales nervous clouds of smoke. Tere looks at Kathy, between the tears drowning her pupils, with certain distrust. What was she doing here? This was a family matter. Nobody had seen her before. Plus, although she looked great, no one could deny that she must be the same age as the Durants. She could be Ishto's mother!

Meanwhile el Ishto continues describing the scene he either lived or imagined. "The selling was bad even though we made up headlines about deaths and such. To make things worse it was Thursday, so no soccer scores to look for; nobody wanted to buy the newspaper."

When people live in a violent society, there comes a time when murders are no longer news but simply daily events. The question is not if people were killed but how many were killed. Waldo added these thoughts to the story he kept writing in his notebook. Ishto is lost in his memories.

"We're not gonna sell shit today!" Cáscara said. "We already wasted half the fucking morning!"

"Well then, why don't you go back to *la champa* and play with el Mono?" el Tripa said.

"Fuck you! You know I don't like that shit, *vos*. You know I do it cuz I have to. Fuck! If we don't sell shit, someone's gonna have to bend over." "*Vos* Ishto, why don't you go there?" He points to a small two-story building at the corner. The property is enclosed by a brick wall with a metal gate that is open. "They know you there. Maybe you can sell something. Those people are loaded and they always read the news and shit."

"Yeah, Ishto *andá*, go. We're gonna see what we can do out here."

"I go in," Ishto says, "and they all seem to know me. They speak funny. The walls are covered with immense paintings. At the top of the stairs is a photo of two people dressed in elegant suits wearing crowns. From above, a voice says, '*Señorita,* miss, please hold my calls. I'm having a meeting with my distinguished guests.' There are more offices upstairs. I sell some newspapers and when I cross the street looking for el Tripa and el

Cascara, a group of people go in and close the door."

Kathy, with their conversation from the previous night fresh in her mind, began to tie up the loose ends. She took the notebook from Waldo, wrote something, and gave the page to don Gustavo. He didn't understand but he accepted the request.

"Ishto," he asked, "before you move away, can you see the address of the building?"
Ishto, still deep inside his memory, turned to scan the building. At one corner he found the numbers. "6-20."

Kathy raised her big eyebrows and flashed her beautiful brown eyes. Don Gustavo didn't understand. Ishto became upset. He started to sweat.
"What do you see, son?" Don Gustavo asked. "Just tell me."
"Smoke, smoke. I believe there's fire. Yes! There's fire, oh my God...from the second floor." His eyelids twitch. "Flames come out through the metal bars on the window! The shouts! The screams!"

"Okay, *cálmate,* settle down, just come back to us. When I count to ten you will open your eyes and everything would be over, I promise. One, two...."
"Janis, when exactly did you three meet on the bus to la Antigua?" "Four, five..." he continued counting.
"January 31, 1980," she said.
"You remember what clothes he was wearing?"
"No."

"Please, Janis, you must remember."

"Una camisa a cuadros," Bob said.

"Was it stained with blood?"

"I don't remember. I still have it in a trunk."

"This man doesn't throw away anything," Janis said.

"Seven, eight...." "I think I know what happened to him, or at least where we can begin the search." "Ten. OK, Ishto, now you can open your eyes."

Chapter 20
Everyone Calls Me Ishto

Ishto rested in his old room in the same house where he'd lived since his adoptive parents settled in the metropolitan area. The small house stood on Arlington Boulevard where every night he could see the stars. It still had the old red desk where he'd done his homework and the shelf just inches above where he'd kept the first videos he'd made when he'd begun to use his camcorder. And under the mattress...the old magazine that had unlocked his teen's desires.

He felt at ease there. He was so exhausted he didn't stop to consider that the flames might return to choke his dream again. Later he would find out what he'd said during the hypnosis session.

Out in the living room, Kathy defined her thesis. She paced as if giving a lecture. "Based on the reaction Ishto had over the holocaust in the Spanish embassy on January 31, 1980, plus the address of the building where he apparently sold newspapers, I'm certain he was either directly involved, was nearby when it happened, or perhaps a loved one died in the fire. He doesn't remember or doesn't want to remember but of course, that's your field of expertise, Doctor Gutiérrez."

"Please call me Gustavo. Well, the possibility exists. For some reason he does not remember but now more than ever I am almost convinced this is more than just a dream."

"We can't force him to remember though," Kathy said.

"Let's remember what happened when he began to see smoke and flames."

"The issue here is that Janis didn't notice anything that would of indicated he'd been in a fire. Although the clothes he was wearing when you guys found him were stained with blood, that doesn't prove he was running away from the fire." Kathy thought for a moment. "It would of been torn or, I don't know...maybe burned or at least smelling like smoke."

Waldo checked his notes. "Ishto said that he or the boy in the dream left the building."

"Yes, and the official reports don't say anything about a boy. Once the police entered the embassy, nobody escaped the place alive except the ambassador and a member of the revolutionary movement. One left the country and the other left this world."

"And what about the three kids selling newspapers?" Tere asked. "Who are they?"

"I think it's him and two of his friends. What do you think, Gustavo? Is it possible that during hypnosis the patient sees things as if they were happening to someone else?"

"Yes. It is called dissociation. Some patients use dissociation to confront a dramatic fact. The story Ishto described is told in first and third person, which makes it more difficult to understand. At this moment I am not ready to say that what he described happened to him or that he saw it happen to somebody else. It is still too early for a diagnosis but I believe these nightmares have their roots in something dramatic that he experienced. Perhaps it is what you referred to, Kathy."

"I believe that although Ishto does not want to accept what happened, he is the boy he sees in his dreams. I believe that there is a battle between two forces raging in his mind. One wants to recover the memory through his dreams while the other convinces his mind that these are just dreams and nothing else. Often it is easier to deal with a dramatic fact by seeing from the point of view of a third person."

"Somebody said something about an *ishto,* right?" Kathy looked at Waldo.

He went through his notes. "Yes, I think it was the one they call Tripa." Waldo read: "Vos *Ishto, why don't you go there?'* and he was directed to a small two story building on the corner that was enclosed by a brick wall and guarded by a metal gate that was open."

"That building could be the Spanish embassy," Kathy said. "At least we have the address. I'll check with an anthropologist friend of mine. She knows this event very well. Janis, who started calling him Ishto?"

"Well, when we arrived at la Antigua and he finally woke up, we asked him his name. He just said, in a Spanish that we barely understood, *'Todos me dicen ishto,* everyone calls me Ishto.'"

"In Guatemala it's common to call children that, although *ishto* is a little derogatory. Perhaps he never knew any better and ended up thinking that was his name."

"Ishto's so screwed, man," Waldo said.

Tere shot him point blank with just a glance while she asked: "But what can we do now?"

"We're gonna have to speak with him again," Kathy said, "perhaps try hypnosis again? What do you suggest, Gustavo?"

The best thing for now is to let him rest. Then we can tell him the story he told us as well as what we think, and leave it up to him to decide. Let me be clear, this is a matter that we must treat very carefully."

"In the meantime, I'll go see the anthropologist who's done a lot of research in Guatemala."

"Gracias, Kathy," Janis said.

As Bob accompanied her to her car, don Gustavo said, "I am going to consult some books."

Waldo continued writing. Then Tere, as if wanting to finish the cycle of collective action, said, "I'm gonna check on him."

Chapter 21
Clash of Civilizations

"Gosh, Kathy, the invasion of the Spaniard Embassy is such a complicated subject."

Thus did Joan Marks, an anthropologist and Kathy's colleague, begin her reply. These friends enjoyed each other's company and a love of the Spanish language. Joan's field of study focused on the pre-Columbian cultures of the Americas. Her investigations had taken her numerous times to the northern part of Guatemala. She joked that in Guatemala they knew her as Juanita. She traveled constantly to the Quiché's region to research lectures. She would undoubtedly help clarify the origin of the man Kathy had begun to see as her....

"Look, Kathy, Guatemala is one of those counties where the Clash of Civilizations hasn't ended. For one thing, the Right as much as the Left have used the natives to obtain their objectives. And don't look at me that way! You know my point of view is pure anthropological."

"Let's take the event in question here. Many of the natives guided to the city by Vicente Menchú didn't know where they were going. They knew they were going to protest against the violence generated by the war between the government and the guerrillas, and sure they wanted to defend their right to keep the land they'd lived on for generations, but they didn't have the basic education nor the ability to communicate to make decisions on their own. Many were monolingual for heaven's sake!"

"They trusted their leader but he was manipulated by revolutionaries. The leader ended up being a follower. Did you know that many went to the city but not all of them invaded the embassy? Yes Kathy, it was an invasion and you know it!" Kathy's ears had turned red; a sign her friend knew meant she was angry. "Some returned to their towns when the demonstrations became violent. These were nonviolent people Kathy! Those who remained were part of the group that invaded the embassy. As you know, some stayed outside watching. They were the same ones who later marched along with the coffins of those who died."

Joan stopped to savor the bittersweet fullness of her wine...bittersweet...as bittersweet as her memories of that Central American country. Her eyes *revolotearon,* glided across the photos hung in her living room. Most of them held the shape of her memories of various indigenous towns of the Americas.

"Guatemala's natives," she continued, "have undergone so much. And yet I'm afraid to say they'll continue suffering if their leaders don't give them their own voice. They must stop importing ideas and find within themselves the common voice that identifies them. You know, when you told me your friend's story, I almost could not believe it. How old was he when his adoptive parents found him?"

"They are not sure. Six or seven." Said Kathy deflating her lungs.
"So now he must be twenty-one or twenty-two, right? Wow! Kathy, how do you manage to hunt these boys?"
"Joan, please."
They both smiled.

"Well, anyways," Joan said, "if you think he was part of the group that *took* the embassy then he's originally from Quiché." Joan sensing her friend's lack of fight had decided to change the term.

"Look, I don't believe he was part of that group because he never sees himself as part of a group...or at least we haven't gotten that far in his memory. The little we know is that he hung out with two other kids. I believe he's somehow involved in the massacre but I don't know exactly how."

"Then the first thing we should do is find out if he's related to someone who died in the embassy. Perhaps a relative died there and that marked his life forever."

"God, Joan, how am I going to find that out? The data on the victims are a little sketchy; they have yet to agree about the number of victims! Some say they were thirty-nine, others say thirty-six. But every document I've read doesn't mention a little boy."

"I know, and that's exactly what intrigues me. I can assure you that David Stoll...you remember him, right? The author of *Rigoberta Menchú and the Story of All Poor Guatemalans* who puts Rigoberta Menchú's version in doubt?"

"Yes, of course."

"Well, according to his investigation...." She stood up and walked to the bookshelf. Still holding the wine glass, she searched for the right section.

"Listen. Stoll speaks of six farmers from Chimel, three from San Pablo Baldío, two from Macalajau and one from the village of Los Plátanos; that's twelve from Uspantán. He mentions three from Chajul, which is a region in Ixil. In addition there were the five activists of the *Comité de Unidad Campesina* plus two from the urban organizations and finally four students from the University of San Carlos. So sixteen farmers from the northern part of Quiché plus eleven activists invaded the embassy. Oh, and let's not forget the ten hostages in the embassy."

"I read the book but to be honest I didn't remember all this data."

"You're getting too close to the subject, and that's affecting your judgment."

Kathy was disappointed. She sensed it would be almost impossible to verify how Ishto, if he were in the embassy during the fire, had arrived there if he didn't remember. "Joan, what was the exact address of the embassy?"

"*A ver permíteme,* let me see." She returned to the shelf and brought back a folder titled *Guatemala.* "I've been collecting information on another case related to the embassy. Don't ask me questions because I'm not gonna say anything else! The building was located in 10ª Street 6-20 *de la Zona* 9."

Kathy became lost in a penumbra of a doubt.

"I understand how you feel, Kathy. This friend of yours could be a relative of any one of these victims. Or he could of been just another visitor in the wrong place at the wrong time."

"But if he was not part of the massacre, why is he so traumatized?"

"There is something else here, Kathy. I don't know what but there's got to be something else. Unfortunately there's nothing else that can be done until he remembers more. I'm sorry but you must realize that what you're trying to do is very difficult."

"You're right, Joan. There's nothing I can do by myself. I'll never be able to help him." She submerged into the sofa."

"Wait a minute! Didn't you say that during the hypnosis he saw himself leaving the building? So he couldn't have been in the fire." "Perhaps he returned and he doesn't remember. I don't know, Joan. Everything is so confusing." "You're not going to give up now, are you? Look, I'm a field anthropologist. You have no idea how many times I've run into multiple closed doors or dead ends. You must have patience and continue digging. Your friend's case looks like an archaeological excavation. You see, when a millenarian object is found; it must be treated very carefully while cleaning. Each detail is important to determine its origin." "I know, Joan, but I don't know if someday we'll be able to arrive at the precise moment that caused the trauma. We were getting close last time but we had to stop because he began to feel really bad. He saw the smoke and the flames and...." "Look, I'm not an expert in hypnotism so I can't tell you how far to push. But I can tell you that when a human being wants to rescue his past, he does whatever is necessary. So tell me when you're going to see him again?" "Soon. He's resting now." "I'm gonna try to find some photos of the building. Perhaps that will help him remember. And I'm gonna take another look at Máximo Cajal's book, how's that called? Gosh, I'm getting old!" "I don't know. You were gonna to let me borrow it but you never--" "*¡Saber quién puso fuego ahí! Who Knows Who Started the Fire There,* What a title, ah? Anyway, if he really wants to know who he is, he will not stop until he finds out. But if he doesn't ...." She took another sip from her glass.

A thick cloud of silence filled the room. Joan smiled trying to offer some comfort. Then with a certain *picardía,* or naughtiness, asked, *"Óyeme,* listen, it must be a great lover, your friend, right? I mean, you're taking it upon yourself to solve this labyrinth."

"Gosh, Joan, you are terrible!"

"I'm just saying...you know you've always been attracted to men without a past."

Kathy answered by making bubbles with the remains of her white wine.

Chapter 22
The Bodies Dance in the Flames of This Man-made Inferno

Little by little, the image of a boy standing before a mirror battling his own reflection with a sword begins to emerge...no...wait a minute.... Two boys are playing. They are identical, though. The front of their house has become the perfect battlefield. The skinny dog has become one's horse. The plucked chicken is the other's eagle. The swords are made of the same wood that keeps the fire burning in the *covacha de la abuela,* grandma's hut. She watches over them from the front door.

The fire barely warms up *la covacha,* slapped hard by the cold wind of the second week of December. Suddenly the noise of jeeps is heard. The military is entering the village. The army of Xibalbá is raising dust, raising fear, raising anguish from those forgotten by history. A shout makes them hurl the swords away and flee inside the rancho. *La abuela* closes the door and begins to shake. *Costales de maiz,* maize sacks, become their protective shield.

What they fear the most happens: the jeep stops in front of the *covacha.* The men strike the door once, twice. Shouts come from Jacinto's *rancho.* Men dressed in camouflage tear down the door. *La abuela* confronts them in an effort to protect her family. A blow from an AK-47 sends her flying across the room. Her grey *trenzas,* braids, wave like the tails of a Quetzal crowning a Mayan priest during a sacrificial ceremony. Then her head strikes the altar and the two candles burned as offerings to the Creator roll away.

Los costales de maiz catch on fire. One of the children runs to his *abuela's* rescue. The other hypnotized by the flames and the dark smoke, watches. The men pull the boy outside by his hair. His screams rip through the smoke as the *covacha* begins to burn. The flames reach the straw ceiling.

The boy behind the *costales de maiz* finds the courage to move and runs to his *abuela*. He pulls her as hard as he can...his eyes are burning...his throat is bleeding. He rolls her across the earthy floor and manages to get her out. He's exhausted. One of the uniformed men sees him.

"¡Parate! ¡Parate hijo'e puta! Stop! Stop! You sonofa bitch!"
There are gunshots. The boy mounts the dust cloud his *caites,* his sandals, make as he flies out of there. When everything finally settles, he's walking without direction. At the end of the road is a truck. He runs to it and hides between stacks of paper, sugarcanes and boxes of tamarind. Through a crack in the truck's wooden fence , he sees a man wiping his ass with a newspaper while whistling. What else could he do with a censured press?
The man finishes... He gets behind the wheel and unknowingly transports a load that doesn't belong to him. The boy closes his eyes and falls asleep in the arms of fear. And he dreams...and he feels...and he starts to see with his eyes closed. He's in the central plaza of the town he no longer belongs to. They have gathered everyone. They still have the other boy by the hair.

"Today we're offering free entertainment!" jokes Tito in the jeep.
"Today, my friends," the Major continues, "we bring you seven traitors to the motherland."

He then proudly describes the treatment they have been given: electrical shocks, extraction of fingernails with sophisticated imported clamps, jabs with needles, et cetera, et cetera, et cetera; basically everything found in a manual of torture. The instructor from the School of the Americas would have given him an A.

Those seven bodies are now no more than masses of swollen meat balancing by feet drenched in blood. The official finishes with an execution-style shot aimed at the temple of bravery. "Listen up. This is what happens to traitors of the motherland who join the rebels."

They bathe the bodies in gasoline. "Who has a match?"

The boy closes the eyes. The guard strikes him on the back of his neck until he opens them again. Everyone in the town wants to close their eyes but they can't. The one dreaming wants to open them but he can't. Those who close their eyes are struck. Everyone must watch the sinister ceremony. There are gunshots...there are blows...there's panic...there's running. Meanwhile, in the center of it all the bodies dance in the flames of this man-made inferno. Their screams burn in the fire that destroys their meat.

Ishto was wrong. The hypnotism session had not exorcised the flames of his dream. As he wakes up bathed in sweat and desperation, he hears the boy who saw the torture ask, "Where's my *abuela?* Where's my brother? Where's God?"

He opened his eyes and saw Tere's face rinsed with weeping. She saw him kicking. She saw him twisting. She saw him suffering. She saw him live or perhaps relive the torture. Enough has been said, so there were no words between them. There were no gestures. They simply stared at each other's eyes and touched one another with their glances.

Chapter 23
A String of Sensations

It's difficult to become a woman when the most yearned for of all references doesn't exist. Learning how to act, how to feel, and even how to behave with a man is often truncated by the search for one's own self.

Thus she'd written in her diary, which had become a string of sensations and feelings she felt important to record. Her father, a man who adored her, couldn't engage in the conversations she needed to hear. He, being a psychologist and all, knew it was very dangerous for a girl to grow up without a mother figure. But no matter how hard he tried, he'd never found another woman who could fill his life the way his beloved Teresa had.

Tere remembered the multiple books her father had given her dealing with the physical changes of one who walks the bridge between a girl and a woman. She was grateful because he tried to make the experience less painful. But nothing he could possible do would lessen the pain of not having her mom during those difficult times. She'd never had many girlfriends. Somehow she'd always felt more comfortable among boys, all the way from Kindergarten to the day she'd met Waldo and Ishto. Her *coquetería* attracted them and her intelligence convinced them to let her join the group.

They never regretted that decision. Working with them brought her so much satisfaction. Her analytical mind offered another angle and enriched the group. Since the day they'd met, Waldo had been the one who wanted to be to her something more than just a friend but Ishto was the one she wanted to move closer to. She'd seen Waldo as a cool guy she'd definitively like to have by her side in an emergency. But Ishto...she'd always fluttered nearer to him like a moth drawn to the light.

And that was how it was for them. The perfect triangle: three vertices united by friendship, understanding and love. The complicated task was to decide where each of them fell...life and its perfect comedy. She'd always been the best student of the three. Love, however, would remain her pending subject. How she wished her mom could be there. How she wished she had a confidant.

Don Gustavo understood this void and so he'd introduced her to the friendly women he'd dated. And she was OK with that but in the end he knew no one could ever occupy the place of her mother. While Ishto twisted with convulsions, she felt compassion and tenderness. And this feeling helped her mind settle. Somehow her heart and brain finally negotiated an agreement. But a doubt still bounced inside of her...would this feeling be reciprocated?

As Ishto started to regain consciousness soaked in sweat, she armed herself with the valor to finally declare her feelings. She was a strong woman; there would be no turning back this time... but once he was wide awake he seemed so fragile, so confused, so lost, that she couldn't do more than just caress him with a pair of eyes that floated in a salty sea. And the moment was forever drowned in her tears.

Chapter 24
Weapon to Indoctrinate

Juan was one of the few who'd managed to stay in school. He attended high school now and looked forward to college. How different he was from the rest of the young guys. They didn't see the point of sitting around listening to someone drone on. Who could blame them? For many there were only two options: *el azadón,* a hoe, or a rifle. And if they didn't comply with this norm, they would generate a third option: the common grave.

This distinction turned Juan into a target for both parties in a conflict polarized by a war more than two decades old. One side saw him as a weapon to indoctrinate from the inside; the other saw him as somebody difficult to intimidate and a potential subversive element.

"Juan, listen to me. Once your mind begins to fly, you can't stay rooted in the ground", one of his teachers had said.

Juan would never know his destiny since the next year he hadn't returned to teach. He, like many others who tried to go beyond 2 + 2 = 4, must have been expelled from the school of life.

In spite of his hectic life, Juan managed to teach Spanish to the region's children. On Market Day while their moms sold goods in the Central Plaza, he sat on the corner by the church to teach a little bit of everything. Some had already began to learn but for others, their *tatas,* dads, had prohibited them from attending. Of everyone who attended, the twins from Chajul were his favorites. It was uncommon to see identical twins in the region; in fact, the only twins he'd heard of were

Hunahpú and Ixbalanqué. They, according to the *Popol Vuh,* the sacred book of the Quichés, descended from Ixquic and Hun-Hunahpú, older brother of Vucub-Hunahpú, who was sacrificed by *los señores de Xibalbá,* the chiefs of Xibalbá. According to the legend, Hunahpú and Ixbalanqué managed to beat *los señores de Xibalbá* and took revenge for the death of their father. Often Juan wondered if the twins were their reincarnation. He knew how badly his people needed someone to fight for them.

Because the twin brothers had this extraordinary connection, they learned faster than the others. When Juan explained something to one of them, the other without being present would learn. When he explained something to both simultaneously, it was as if he had taught both of them twice. Unfortunately, this unusual connection also created problems. When one of them suffered or was hurt, the other felt it.

What began as a fascination soon became affection. Somehow Juan became something of an older brother to them. They were orphans, a common thread that connected many children of the region. Juan often worried that this shared affection would create consequences. He'd already begun to embrace situations that encouraged change in the region.

The connection with one of the twins, the one who'd survived the horrible public torture a month before, had become narrower now that the other one had disappeared. He tried to push him away but he would return. The boy, who lived with his now nearly blind and mute *abuela* due to the head injury she suffered that day, needed somebody. And that somebody was Juan.

But he couldn't leave the Movement; especially now that he was even more convinced the Cause needed members who would act on behalf of the vulnerable ones. When the trip to the capital was organized, Juan told the boy he was going to go visit some relatives and he couldn't come because he had to care for his *abuela*. He was surprised later when he found him sleeping between paper bulks at the back of the rental bus.

Once they arrived in the town of San Carlos, he struggled with whether to leave him behind or take him to the demonstrations. Both options were dangerous. Taking him back was not an option because they could not make that trip alone. Even back in Uspantán he'd noticed someone following him. He feared that somebody would recognize the kid as his friend and would hurt him.

He managed to hide the boy from the leaders throughout their stay. It wasn't difficult since they all slept in classrooms on the third level of a building. Tactical meetings were carried out in the second floor but would never include anyone who wasn't a leader; plus those from the countryside never met directly with the student leaders from the capital. That was don Vicente's duties; as their leader, he would later tell them which steps to follow. Some students met with *campesinos,* farmers, to indoctrinate them. It was Juan's job to explain to the comrades what the chat had been about.

"*A ver vos, Juan.* Hey, Juan," a member of his group once asked, "*si estos de adeveras nos qu'eren ayudar, ¿po'qué nos hablan en su lengua vos?* If these guys really wanna help us, how come they speak to us in their language, *vos?*" The meetings were conducted in Spanish.

When the announcement finally came that they would demand their rights inside the Spaniard Embassy, the participants were excited. They thought their voices would finally be heard. Nobody bothered to explain what an embassy was and much less what or who that so-called Spain happened to be.

What was Juan going to do with the *patojo,* the kid, attached to his *morral,* bag? Perhaps it would had been better to have sent him back with the group that returned to the town, he thought as his *caites* or sandals crunched atop broken glass. But then he wasn't even sure they had made it back safe and sound. He didn't want the kid by his side but at least that way he could protect him.

He'd been wrong. Early that morning a comrade had handed him a blanket he was to hang at the *Subida,* the place they were going, once the order was issued. He also gave him a bandana to cover his face. The chants began: *¡El pueblo... unido... jamás será vencido!, The people... united... will never be conquered!*

They marched in small groups that would not call any attention. One of the leaders saw him gripping the kid's little hand. When he approached them, Juan shielded the boy with his body. He thought he was going to be taken away or he would be told to leave the boy behind. But the guy said, "Once we get to the *Subida,* make sure you carry him in your arms. It'll be great if the press can see him."

Chapter 25
Take the Facts, String Them Together with Poetry and Create Stories

Waldo swallowed saliva to see if the hammer, the anvil and the stirrup bones in his ears would come to terms with the pressure created by flying. He hated flying because sooner or later his ears would react. Kathy sat on his right with her eyes closed listening to a Lila Downs. He read the artist's name despite the tiny dimensions of the iPod Nano's screen. He'd never heard of the singer but thought that somebody with a name like that was destined to be an artist.

Taking advantage of the fact that Kathy seemed to be asleep, he admired her beauty. The black hair fought to free itself from the ponytail forcing it back into a barrette. The eyelashes flirted up like silk wings. She had thin lips and applied lipstick millimeters beyond their edges to make them look fuller. Yeah, definitively that woman has come to know herself to perfection.

He noticed the little gold medallion that raised and lowered along with her breath. When he was on the verge of leaning forward to read the inscription, she said without opening her eyes, "It's bad manners to take advantage of people while they sleep."

His soul spun out of the airplane from the vertigo of having been caught with its hand in the cookie jar. "I'm...I'm...I'm sorry, I thought you were...."

"It's OK. I wasn't. I just like closing my eyes when I listen to Lila. Have you heard of her?"

"No."

"I think you'd like her. She's like the three of you. She lives between two worlds and somehow has no problem crossing the bridge back and forth, back and forth."

"Cool... hey Kathy, I wanna thank you for helping us with Ishto."

"You're very welcome. Although I've the impression that not everyone is happy with me being here."

"Huh if you're talking about Tere, don't worry. She'll come around. It's just sister's jealousy, you know."

"Oh, it is jealousy, I agree, but not the sister's kind."

"C'mon, Kathy. Why would you say that? She's like a sister to us."

"Are you sure, Waldo?"

Beautiful, intelligent and intuitive, he thought. Waldo had yet to find out that Ishto had already beat him to the punch and decided to give it a shot. "So...what makes a woman as beautiful as you play detective with a crazy trio like us?"

He ran his tongue across his upper lip and left its tip massaging the other corner. It was his shout to war. It was his version of a peacock unfolding its feathers ready to mate.

"Wow, you and Ishto! As a friend of mine use to say, *no dejan santo parado,* hit on everyone."

"Not everyone. Only the ones worth the trouble."

"Well then, I would suggest you step on the break paddle, pal. We must direct our energy to helping your friend, remember?"

"Well, a deflection would not be so bad."

"Listen, Waldo, why don't you flirt with that notebook you haven't touched since we began the flight?"

Ouch! Love is indeed a battlefield and the only sure thing is a loss for the one who chooses not to fight. "I don't have the muses with me. I was gonna bring them in my carry-on but TSA forced me to put them in the luggage. You know, some of them are sharp."

"I see. So then tell me, when are you are gonna let me see something you've written?"
"I don't show a work in progress."
"Well, we humans are a work in progress. Imagine if we'd refuse to show ourselves until we were complete."

He found her slight accent when she spoke Spanish fascinating.
"I still can't figure out why neither one of you took at least one course with me," she said. "I think you two only choose the easy ones."
"Never. Well, you know, there are times when one has the urgency and takes whoever is avai--"
"Waldo, I'm talking about courses."
"Oh, sorry.... Well, I dunno .... Hey, Kathy, can I ask you something?"
"Wow! I'm scared now 'cuz up until this moment you have not requested permission, and let me tell you there were moments when you should have."
"I am sorry. I didn't mean to offend you."
"I'm just kiddin'. So tell me what you wanna ask."
"Do you think we can help Ishto? This is kinda messed up, isn't it?"

"Well, after all that's happened and studying the data carefully, I believe his life is definitely connected to the holocaust at the Spaniard Embassy. That's why I was so happy when he said he wanted to return to Guatemala to search for his past. I believe the hypnosis finally touched bottom. I still can't figure out if he was inside or only present at the event but it definitely traumatized him."

"And what are we gonna do when we get there?"

"I've a friend, he's guatemalteco, who I've known for a long time."

Waldo *frunció la boca,* made a gesture like he was sucking on a lemon.

"He can take us places that can shine some light," she said. "The first thing we ought to do is show him the newspapers from that time to see if Ishto remembers something. I believe his mind is on the verge of remembering; it only needs a little push, you know? It could be a place, an article, a friend, or simply a building. I'm not sure but I have faith…. So tell me, what do you mean you don't have the muses with you? Don't tell me you ran out of subjects to write about."

"I don't know, Kathy. There are times when the well just dries out, you know."

"You've read about the civil war in Central America, right?"

"Yes, of course. I've read a lot about the Compromised Literature and all that."

"Good. So you're telling me what happened there doesn't inspire you to write about it."

"I prefer fiction, Kathy."

"You know, let me tell you something. I've been involved with many political movements. I've written books and a few articles on those issues and in retrospect, I believe that one of the problems we have is that our writings have been," here she used her left forefinger to tick off the fingers of her right hand, "investigations full of cold numbers, political pamphlets or testimonials. I believe it's necessary to write more literature about these subjects. You understand? Literature based on reality but that doesn't leave aside the artistic beauty great Latin American novels have. Something in the neighborhood of what your compatriot Ramirez does in Nicaragua, you see what I'm saying?"

"Sure but don't you think that that would be like betraying the memory of those who had been affected?"

"No, because you would not be creating a new history. You would be stringing real facts together and reconstructing their history. You're not gonna lie, you're gonna poetize the facts."

"Las verdades mentirosas y las mentiras verdaderas."

" What?"

"The facts hidden in the fiction, and the fiction hidden in the facts." That was an expression that a literature professor used in her class. It belongs to a Latin American writer, who uses it to explain his writings."

"Good. At least you had one good professor at AU."

"Oh, there are good professors at AU, you just have to look for them. *De todo hay en la viña del señor como dicen por allí,* like they say, it takes all kinds to make a world."

"I'm going to lend you this book." She shuffled through her handbag. "I know you're not Guatemalan but--"

"It don't matter though. I've read a lot about Guatemala. My admiration for its people lead me to *el loco del Ishto,* to this crazy one."

She smiled. "Here. You'll find examples of massacres committed against Guatemalan and Central American natives. They give details but not so many you'll feel restricted. So take the facts, string them together with poetry and create stories. I don't know you that well but what I've seen so far and what Ishto has told me tells me you are very sensible. You, as a writer, will find in sociology books the ingredients you yearn for to begin telling the other history, the one that escaped historians. And now let me rest my eyes for a moment, and please don't you bother me with your glance or as you would put it when you are inspired, don't spill the lava of your pupils on my body."

He was surprised and a little awestruck with admiration. She closed her eyes and enjoyed her moment of poetic inspiration. He wrote down the phrase and as he turned the pages of the book, he heard Ishto talking to Tere two rows ahead of them. By the time the announcement prepared passengers for landing, he had already finished writing the rough draft of *The Signal*.

Chapter 26
The Signal

It was March thirteen. A day just like any other, or perhaps not. Maria got up at four ground the maize and now she was about to cook tortillas on the little *comal*, the flat griddle, for the lunch of the one who was washing his face and preparing to sow.

Los patojos, the children, were still dreaming on the *petate*. But the two old enough to work–ages eight and nine--were getting ready. They knew that once their *tata* finished his black bean soup with *chirmol*, salsa, and coffee made from grilled tortillas, they will go to the field and won't return until dusk.

The mother served their breakfast just like their *tata's* and went for water. The cracked *tinaja*, earthen jar, dissipated the dust her little hops raised. She looked up at the volcano's zenith. It was completely covered by clouds; according to the belief, today would be a day of peace. When she went back to the hut, they were already gone.

Later she would know that that was the last time she would ever see them.

Nine o'clock. Time to go to the river and wash some clothes. She held a child at each hand and one attached to her back by the typical *perraje,* the textile she wove herself. Her hips moved left to right as she skillfully juggled the basket of dirty clothes on her head. She met there with other women. Some washed clothes in the river with their *corte,* skirt tied up around their knees. Others spread them on the rocks to dry while others bathed half-naked with their little children by their sides. Deep in the forest was an *alux*, an elf, who enjoyed watching them play in the clear water.

At one o'clock Maria made her way back to the village to help her mother-in-law clean the maize, ferment the *chicha,* an alcoholic drink, and weave *güipiles*. Later they would cook dinner together.

Just over an hour later while she watched her children pretend to be Hunahpú and Ixbalanqué, the twins from Mayan mythology, shots, screams, and the *tan, tan, tan, tan* of church bells announced terror. It was the signal, they must leave. The army of *Xibalbá*, the place of darkness, had entered the village.

The gown of clouds along the volcano's zenith had ripped and it was completely uncovered. She must get her *patojos* and flee to the mountains. Everyone knew what to do. There was no need to say anything. Her mother-in–law, however, refused to leave. The *Achís*, the people from this region, had lived most of this war running from one place to the other. This time she would not run. Maria managed to hide her in one corner. She covered her with some sacks and begged her not to move. She would return with the *patojos* as soon as the bells tolled again.

Two hours passed and the signal was not given. She prayed that God not allow Chepe, her husband, and her kids come home early. An hour later *tan, tan, tan, tan,* the bells announced the army's retreat. From the place where they always hide they saw smoke rising from the village. That was not unusual since the army always burned *ranchos* out frustration when they were unable to punish the subversives.

This time it was a setup. Someone from the village had told the army about the signal before he was executed, and they gave the false signal. The army had not left. They hid around the central plaza where villagers always gather after these emergencies. The moment the army saw them, they started shooting.

One after another fell: children, elders, animals, everyone. And those who would not fall were brought down by blows or slashed with machetes. Heads fell, arms fell, bodies fell, lives fell into the labyrinth of the unknown. A mountain of disfigured bodies arose. A stream of blood emanated from it and the *río negro*, the black river, found its way to the hydroelectric Chixoy.

They all died victims of the army, all of them. Everyone except the old woman hiding under the sacks. She died from panic. She died from desolation. She died little by little. One by one her senses stopped working. First it was the sense of sight and she could no longer see what was happening outside. Then it was the sense of smell followed by taste, and she could no longer smell or taste the blood that ran between the rocks outside. Finally it was the sense of hearing and she could no longer hear the moans, the guns, or recriminations that came without reason. She lost the ability to talk and couldn't scream. She, with nothing more than her imagination and a sense of touch, imagined the little bodies of her grandchildren hugging their mother while bullets drilled their bodies. The old woman died feeling the pain of her family.

At that moment, she remembered that some time ago a group of young people dressed in olive green had talked to them about the revolution. Nobody from the village heard their plea. This was a pacifistic town. Now she wondered if that had been a mistake.

While her heart offered the last *tan, tan, tan, tan* beats she rose into the skies. From there she attended the exhumation of the victims. Eleven years had passed since the massacre and just last year some had celebrated the yell of *¡tierra!* land! given by someone named Rodrigo from a Spaniard ship. That yell became a premonition for the burial of the great cultures that lived in the so-called New Continent.

Among the people who attended the exhumation, she recognized her son and the two grandchildren who had survived. Chepe's face was marked with deep anguish. The older grandchild was a young man and his brother was still carrying the *morral*, the woven haversack, she had made for him. Quetzals decorate each side. The three of them clung to the remains of their family. They were crying and yet they were smiling because the world would finally know what had taken place in the village. She heard the *tan, tan, tan, tan* of the bells but this time it came with a beautiful light that surrounded her. Her daughter-in-law and her three grandchildren opened their arms. And she thought, *Perhaps now I will finally understand why… tan, tan, tan….*

Chapter 27
The Regretful Gringo

Almost fifteen years had passed since she'd last seen Pablo. He had changed so much. They had arranged for him to pick them up at the Aurora International Airport but it took her a while to recognize him. She saw him between relatives hugging adventurers who'd flown in from *el Norte*. Some arrived well-dressed and carrying lots of luggage that proved their success in Uncle Sam's land. Others returned with faces stained by disappointment and failure.

She hoped to see that skinny guy of white complexion and light brown *colochitos*, curly hair, in the eternal black *playera*, or t-shirt, and faded jeans. The eternal gentleman who always carried a pair of red bandanas in his back pocket: one to cover his face and the other to offer his companion. Even in difficult circumstances, he'd always been a gentleman. But when this heavy man wearing a light blue buttoned-up long sleeve dress shirt approached her wearing an immaculately white *playera* underneath and a pair of navy blue trousers, the image shattered.

She tried to disguise her disillusion but that was the final period to the revolutionary novel left unfinished in some forgotten drawer over a decade ago. He, on the other hand, found her as beautiful as the last time he'd seen her. The lines around her eyes lent a mysterious glow to the face that was always ready to offer a smile.

As soon as he had the chance, he got on 7ª Avenue and stayed on it for the entire trip. When they passed by the site of the tragedy in zone 9, they both stared into each other's eyes and kept silent to honor the victims.

Through the window, his forgotten history gave Ishto a warm welcome. For the first time, he felt the presence of the half for whom he longed. He felt complete, he felt at ease, he felt ready to unearth the truth but still was fearful about discovering what had happened. It was rush hour but Pablo wanted the visitors to see the metropolis. They passed by Banco de Guatemala, the country's central bank, the Plaza Central, the Cathedral, went by 5ª Street and then to 12th Avenue until they found the street where he and his family lived.

Juan Chapín Avenue sat on the outskirts of *Cerrito del Carmen,* Carmen's Hill. Kathy and Pablo talked the entire trip and touched on almost every subject. Kathy noticed that in spite of Pablo's physical change, inside he preserved the young noble joker. His gestures were similar to Ishto's, although their physical appearance could not have been more different. Ishto with his thick, black, straight hair and his dark complexion seemed more authentic to this region than Pablo. But both were Guatemalan, one completely convinced of it and the other seeking the lost link that would connect him to the land of the Mayans.

The group clicked almost immediately and the jokes kept flowing. Pablo kept calling Ishto *el gringo arrepentido,* the regretful gringo. Curiously when he'd first met Kathy, that's exactly what he'd called her: *la gringa arrepentida.* She'd arrived at a crucial time in his life. If not for her, he would hate all *gringos.* With her he discovered the gray tones to the love-hate relationship between both countries.

Back then Kathy fought her government for supporting the butcher dictators throughout Latin America; he fought the butchers supported by her government. This common cause joined them and love united them. With her, destiny gave him a reason to forget his aged hatred. Nevertheless, he continued fighting this feeling.

"Oíme vos Ishto, con ese apodo la verdad que no podés decir que no sos guatemalteco vos. Listen, Ishto with that nickname, there's no way you can deny being Guatemalan, *vos."*

The three of them noticed that peculiar Guatemalan rhythm that made them smile.
"No pues pa'que negarlo... vos, no, there's no use denying it...*vos."* He added the *"vos"* like someone carefully testing the water with one foot. He began throwing maize grains into the soil to see if they stuck. Later the harvest would come.

"Me encanta venir a Guate. I love visiting Guatemala," Kathy said.
"Yes," Pablo said. "Unfortunately that love doesn't include coming to see me."
"Don't say that, Pablo. Whenever I come, you're out in a trip."
"You are a retailer?" Tere asked.
"No. Well, more or less. I mean, I distribute textbooks and notebooks donated by nongovernmental agencies, what you guys call NGOs. The salary is not that great but at least there's payment. And what do you two do? I say you two because I already *chotié* that Waldo works for the CIA, I mean 'cuz of all that writing, you know."

"*Chotié,*" Kathy repeated. "I'd already forgotten that word. So Guatemalan."

"What's that mean?" Ishto asked.

"To see, to notice, or to catch someone in the act," Pablo said in English. "For instance, you can tell someone, '*Ayer te chotié en la Sexta,* hey, I saw you yesterday walking down the Sexta. That's short for Sixth Avenue, it's a crowded place were you can buy almost everything. Perhaps we will drive by it today. Or you can also confront someone by saying, '*Ya te chotié que vos andás tras los huesos de mi traida.* I noticed you're after my *traida.*'"

"Girlfriend," Kathy added.

The outburst of laughter flew through the windows.

"If you find yourself *a traido,* Tere, you would hear that phrase very often because you're very *chula.*"

"That means pretty, right?" Tere asked, more for reassurance than for translation.

"Of course." Pablo admired her self-confidence.

"Well, anyways, we have a video production company. We make commercials for local television."

"DeLos Reyes Productions," Ishto added. "Waldo is the writer of the group."

"That's right!" Pablo said. "I think Kathy mentioned that when she said you guys were coming. Now I understand why Waldo is somewhere else. Writers are like that."

Ishto wondered if Kathy had also mentioned that they were more than friends.

From the back Waldo said, "If Américo Vespucio had not written what he saw, this place would not be called America."

"Well said, Waldo." Pablo nodded. "You *Nicas,* Nicaraguans, certainly know how to blow it out of the park. Look, this is downtown. You guys can come see movies here. This week they're showing movies from Latin America. For the International Film Fest, you know."

"We have a Latin-American Film Fest in Washington, too. It's pretty good."

"I don't know about the censorship these days but there must be good *licas*...that mean films in Chapín." He smiled.

"Oh, look, the National Palace," Kathy sighed.

"So many memories, no?"

"Yes."

"Remember *La Huelga de Dolores?*" And just like that Pablo started chanting its hymn. "*Mata-sanos practicantes.*"

Kathy didn't join him.

"*Mata-sanos practicantes,*" Pablo started again, looking at her with surprised. How could she have forgotten the hymn of the San Carlos University's students to Huelga de Dolores?

Sensing his disappointment, she dug deeper in her memory and unearthed an image of herself on a *carroza,* a float, next to a drawing of Reagan dressed in white and red stripped trousers and a starry top hat hiding AK-47s under his blue coat. The word *"Contras"* written across.

"*Mata-sanos practicantes,*" Pablo repeated, begging Kathy with his broken voice to remember.

"*Del emplasto fabricantes,*" she continued with the happiness and fascination of one who has discovered fire.

"*Güisachines del lugar,*" Pablo continued.

Together they shouted, "*Estudiantes: de la patria derrengada riamos. Ja! Ja!*"

They laughed remembering the way they had been, and feeling again what they lived through. Happy to see that their shared past united them still.

The three in the back didn't understand. The two in the front didn't want to explain because some things can't be explained, just felt. And to be able to feel them, one must have lived them.

"What is that *Huelga de* what?" Ishto asked.

"*La Huelga de Dolores,*" Kathy answered. "It's basically a humorous parade where the San Carlos University students, San Carlos is the only public university here in Guate, voice their disapproval to corrupt politicians." She turned to Pablo. "You know Pablo, I often wonder if it was worth the trouble. I mean, so much sorrow and pain."

"Of course it was worth the trouble, Kathy! At least now the one who lives in the presidential house doesn't wear a military uniform."

"I know, Pablo, but so many *compañeros,* friends, were lost."

"At least thanks to them their children can breathe a little more freedom, Kathy. Now it's their call to fight with other arms. Alright, guys, we're here!"

"Ay, the Juan Chapín. This place has always enchanted me. Everything seems perfect. The Cerrito del Carm...what happened?" Kathy asked as soon as the estate came into view.

"They had to build that ugly high fence around it. You know *las maras,* gangs, are terrible here."

"You know, guys," Kathy said with the excitement of a teen, "it used to be open so people could throw races to the top. There's a little beautiful church all the way up there. So tell me, Pablo, do couples still set up dates there?"

"Please don't go there. Whenever I see Laurita, I see myself killing someone."

Kathy laughed. "Don't say that. What makes you think you're the only gentleman who ever wandered this beautiful country...Laura is a pretty name."

"Yes, we both liked it."

"Oye, listen, I can't believe I finally gonna meet the only woman whose trap worked!!"

They both smiled.

"Well, actually, she's out. As a matter of fact, they're both out. They went to Antigua to see her parents."

"Is everything OK?"

"Her dad is sick. He's old, you know."

"Is it serious?"

"I talked to him yesterday and he was feeling better already. They've been really good to us."

"I'm glad to hear that. I hope he gets well soon."

"Pues, primero Dios, with God's will. I miss my Laurita so much."

He parked on one side of the street in front of the house. He still lived in the house where he'd grown up; his mother had left it to him when she died. He showed them their rooms. The men would share one and the women would share a second. Ishto and Waldo looked at each other's disappointment.

"Or if you guys prefer another arrangement," Pablo said.

"No, Pablo, this is fine," Kathy said. "You've already done enough by saving us the trouble of booking a hotel and transportation at the last moment."

"Good, then. I'll let you guys get settled. I have to go now but I'll be back soon." Before he left, he turned around and said, *"Mi casa es tu casa."*

Chapter 28
They had both been wrong

The soft light of the beautiful moon painted the concrete rooftop they both knew so well with brush strokes taken from *The Starry Night.* Between them, the bottle of red wine he had bought after hearing about her visit. They looked towards el Cerrito del Carmen separated only by the little round cedar table holding taquitos from the diner at the end of the street that after all these years still taste the same. She dipped one in hot sauce and as soon as she took the first bite, confetti from a taquito fried to perfection showered her light orange silk blouse.

"Nobody makes taquitos like she does."
"No, no one."
"How many times did we sit here with our comrades to chat?"
"And to send smoke signals," she added with a smile that masked her embarrassment.
"I miss those days, Kathy. They were difficult days sure but at least the youth then joined forces for a cause. Now there's no alliance. They all walk scattered around without belonging to nothing. Sometimes a concert or a soccer match or some shit like that gets them together but that's it. It's so disappointing!"
"Well, at least they don't have to live what our generation lived, Pablo. Bombing *a la carte*, police sirens so loud we couldn't hear ourselves think!"
"*Estas chula,* Kathy."
"*Jah!* Here comes Don Juan." She leaned back in the beach chair.
"What happened to us, Kathy?"

"Well...we put our cause over everything else. Relationships need time, and we were always so busy in other things.... And then I had to go."

"What do you think would've happened...if I--?"

"No, Pablo." She was terse. "Don't ask that. Remember Laurita would not exist if you hadn't stayed here.... Remember we were in two different situations. This was not my country. I could leave anytime but you, you loved this country more than you loved...." She hesitated, juggled the pronouns in her mind and finally whispered, "Yourself."

"You're right. I always thought my duty was to fight for my country, seek equality, fight for my people, and now look at me. I'm tired of fighting and so frustrated to see that those who didn't fight are the ones better off. Believe me, there are times I wish I could reverse my decisions. I don't know...maybe make it more about me, about my education. I see you, a doctor and all, and I regret not having continued school to see where it would of taken me. When I was going to El Central I spent more time outside the classroom than inside. I would 'F' tests left and right and I didn't give a 'f'.... I would skip school and--"

"Yes, Pablo, but you didn't skip school to enjoy yourself, remember? You did it to go to a demonstration, to fight for your ideals!"

"Well, the result was the same, damn it! I never thought about my future. I always thought the cause would triumph and now that I see that the jobs are given to university graduates who don't know shit. It makes me so mad at the fucking system but above all, I'm pissed at myself!"

The silence let their breathing dance with the sounds of crickets in love.

"You know? I just got my GED...I had so much fun going back to school."

"You were always very intelligent, Pablo. You belonged inside the school not outside fencing the fucking tear gas bombs!"

The scream of sirens was heard across the distance and soon the breeze dragged it away into the thickness of the night.

"Fuck melancholy!" Kathy said. "Let's toast in honor of the graduate!"
They raised their glasses and the clink of them meeting transported them back to the night when, drawing loops of smoke on this very same roof, they had wept at the death of their best friend, kidnapped then mutilated by the police. The group was marked. That night she decided to go back to the United States and he decided to go underground.
"Come with me, Pablo," she'd said. "We're gonna fight against the enemy from the inside."
"No, Kathy. I can't leave the cause."
"I'm not asking you to leave the cause, simply the method. Don't you see they're killing all the brains? When the cause triumphs, who's going to govern? Come with me!"

He'd thought she was leaving him. She'd thought he didn't love her enough to begin a life with her. But they had both been wrong. There on the cold rooftop they remembered seeing each other for the last time on the platform at the Time Train Station waiting to board their assigned cars. Then their images had faded into the crowd like statuettes in a Monet.

That long-ago night two plastic cups had been suspended in the air; tonight they held crystal glasses. But the result was still the same: she staring at her own reflection and he staring at his. After so many years they still didn't see each other. He wanted to confess that he'd grown tired of counting the nights face-up on this same spot counting the stars and thinking of her. He wanted to confess that for too long he'd drenched his memory after the spasms of the fruit of his pain gushed over him. He wanted to recite the last verse of the poem he had discovered by chance.

But he couldn't. His pride wouldn't let him find the courage Batres Montufar had to say, *Sin lucha, sin afán y sin lamento, sin agitarme en ciego frenesí, sin proferir un solo, un leve acento, las largas horas de la noche cuento. ¡Y pienso en ti!,* Without struggle, without emulation and without lamentation, without waving myself in blind frenzy, without dropping only one, a light accent, the long hours of the night I count. And I think of you!

She heard everything; she felt everything because she too had found him penetrating the wet vertex of a fleeting dream. But she pretended not to hear. She pretended not to feel. She blamed the reason. He blamed his principles and once again he decided to behave like a gentleman and not start something he couldn't, he wouldn't finish. He preferred to cling to reality and joked, "You're bathed in taco."
"Yes! Look at me! I'm a mess!"

And the sad memories which had hovered in the air became Kamikazes of time and one by one collided against the mountains of oblivion. Amid the dust of the explosions, she too decided to turn the page of the memory book and said, "Then what? Are you going to help discover what really happened to my friend or have you already stopped looking for the truth between the lies?"

"No way! Kathy."

"As a matter of fact, tomorrow we're gonna see an acquaintance of mine who can give us more info on the people who took the embassy. I was thinking we could send Waldo to the newspaper archive at the Central Library for information on the taken. He, being a writer and all, must know how to research, right?"

"I hope so."

"I really think we should take Ishto to the actual place to see if he remembers something. Perhaps being there will trigger his memory."

"Hmmm...I don't know if that would be a good idea. We don't know how he's gonna react. Besides--"

"Well, he must be strong. A man is nothing without his memories. Who would I be without mine? It doesn't matter what's hidden in his past. He has to know what really happened!"

"You're right. So when was that film they went to see supposed to be over?"

"I'm not sure but they should be on their way by now."

Chapter 29
¿Qué Quemazón? What Fire?

"We should find out when *La Casa de Enfrente* is," Waldo said as they left the movies. His right hand was lost inside a paper bag searching for the last of the popcorn. The rest started laughing.

"Well, perhaps that'd inspire you to start writing so we can finally shoot our damn film!" Ishto said. "The way we're going we'll never shoot anything!"

He looked at Tere for approval.

"You don't know what I'm working on, man!"

"That's exactly my point, bro'! No one knows what the fuck you're working on!"

"OK kids," Tere said, "settle down. Let's see, who's gonna get us a cab?"

"I don't see anything."

"What if we take the bus?"

"Sure! Which one, genius?"

"I dunno."

"Very well then, let's just start walking. I'm sure one would show up sooner or later. I think it'd be hard to catch one here with everyone leaving the theater. Let's go!"

"How are we gonna start walking if we don't even know where we're going?"

"Look, Pablo said that la Sexta was like the main street so if we keep on it we'll find something."

They reached the Plaza Mayor.

"Hey, you guys think that Kathy and Pablo had...you know, back in the day...something more than just a friendship?"

"I don't know. I see them *como...compenetrados,* you know."

"Well there you go then. The word says it all, doesn't it? *Con pene.*"

"Waldo, easy man."

"C'mon, man, was just a joke. Why so sensitive?"

"Cut it out!"

"Geez. I should have stayed at that place we just passed...the porn looked interesting."

"Look there," Tere said. "There's a cab. Taxi! Taxi!"

"Nice cab you got us, Tere! I don't think this is gonna make it. Look. It's blowing smoke, rattles and shit, I feel like a tourist in la Habana."

All of a sudden, the shaking stopped. "Don't worry, kids," the driver said. "I'll start it right away."

The cabbie tried once, again, and once again. Nothing.

"Listen, do you wanna us to give it a push?"

"We can try, kid, but I'm afraid he's dead."

"But...what can we do?"

"Should we call them and see if they can pick us up?"

"Hay no! *Que pena!* I'd be embarrassed to call!" Tere said. "Look, sir, I think your *chatarrita,* clunker, is done for the night and maybe even for life so why don't you just tell us how to get to el Cerrito del Carmen?"

"Oh just keep going straight on Twelve."

"Is it far away?"

"Not too far, no."

"OK, Ishto, pay him and let's get going."

"Why me? You better get the next one, man!"

They started walking. They passed a group of guys hanging out at a corner as one of them made a phone call.

"How far can this freaking place be!"

"I don't know, you guys, but I didn't get a good vibe from those guys we just walked by."

Suddenly a group of men cut in front of them.

"*Cáiganse con la lana y no hay pedo,* hand us the money and you'll be fine."

By then the other group had come up behind them. They were surrounded.

"*¡El dinero pues, puta!* I said, hand me the fucking money!"

Waldo was completely gone. He'd just blipped out mentally. Tere clung to his hand and Ishto...Ishto refused to stop. He just kept walking.

"*¿Bueno vos cerote, ¿estás sordo o qué putas?* What's wrong with you, motherfucker? Are you deaf or something?" asked the leader from the dark side of the street.

"We got no money, man." Just leave us alone."

"No money? Let's see."

One of them started searching Ishto's back pocket. Ishto threw him to the ground.

"This motherfucker is loaded!" The entire hive of wasps fell on him.

"Ishto!" Tere screamed.

Waldo had a knife to his throat. He couldn't move. Blood trickled down his shirt. Once they had taken Ishto's wallet, they started kicking him.

"Here it is, Tripa." One of the gang handed him the wallet.

That nickname buzzed in Ishto's ears. By pure instinct, he shouted, "*Tripa! Tripa!*"

The beating stopped. The leader ordered Ishto to stand up. He left the shadows and stepped into the tenuous light of the street. He was a skinny and scruffy young man whose face showed traits of excesses. Waldo was glued to Tere, focused on protecting her without paying any attention to the knife piercing his neck.

"*¿Vos maje me conocés o qué,* do you know me?"

"*¿Y vos a mí,* how about you...do you know me?"

"*¿Quién putas sos,* who the fuck are you?"

"*Yo soy el Ishto,* I am Ishto."

"*¿Quién?* Who?"

Ishto approached him as if he really knew him. Two gang members stepped between them. Ishto wasn't sure but the nickname told him something.

"*Vos me conoces a mí,* you know me... I can feel it," Ishto said.

Could it be possible that this now dirty, beat-up guy was the same kid he'd sent to the Embassy to sell newspapers before the fire? In the month they'd been together, he had grown fond of him and had even protected him from el Mono.

"*Vos, devolvéles sus mierdas.* You, give them back their shit," he ordered.

Nobody understood but they all obeyed.

"I don't know you! You hear me?" Tripa said. "*Vámonos muchá,* let's go!"

The entire gang tried to understand what was happening.

"*Yo a vos te conozco,* Tripa, I do know you," Ishto said.

"*¡Ya dije que nos fueramos puta!* I said, let's go!"

"No, Tripa. *Necesito hablar con vos,* I need to talk to you."

"*Ya te dije que yo a vos no te conozco.* I told you I don't fucking know you!"

"*Y entonces, ¿por qué me devolvés mis mierdas?* So then why you give me back my shit!" Ishto was now the one threating the leader.

"Fue mala onda mía dejarte en ese relajo, it wasn't cool for me to leave you in that mess. *Yo pensé que te habías muerto, pero ya que te salvaste ahora estamos a mano,* I thought you died but since you survived, I'm now making it even. I own you nothin'."

"*¿De qué estás hablando?* What are you talking about?"

"*¡De la quemazón, pues!* The fire, you idiot!"

"*¿Qué quemazón?* What fire?"

Police sirens were approaching. Someone had finally taken the trouble to inform the authorities precisely when they were least needed. The men holding Waldo and Tere threw them to the ground and fled. Tripa did the same. Ishto ran after them. Tere shouted for him. Waldo held onto her so she could not follow. The lights of the police car blinded them. *La mara* was swallowed by the darkness.

Chapter 30
Why Two of Everything and Not One of Nothing?

The desolated *abuela* Ixcanil does not want to eat. She spends time and time again weaving and weaving in the labyrinth where she had been trapped since she lost one of the two. Her meal of black bean soup with scraps of tortilla serves as a lagoon for a flock of flies that splash in the forgotten feast. The black liquid in the clay bowl reflects the wood pole lodged in the ground that facilitates the task. She's about to finish the new *perraje*.

This, like the last one, shows a couple of something together but separated by emptiness. It's always the same *le motif:* a pair of flowers, a couple of quetzals, a couple of *ceibas,* a couple of creepers, a couple of something. It reproduces all that was destroyed that afternoon when the army of Xibalba stole away half of her life and the whole of her conscience. The hunchback hides the head fixed in the textile and nothing else. The fabric is her world that begins and ends with each loom.

The *tuntún* that once adorned her long hair lies tangled in the ash-colored strings spilled across the back of her colorful *güipil*. Her deformed and bony fingers thrust and strike multicolored strands that give life to her creation and tell her story. Who listens? Who cares? She continues searching for the faces of the two who once were but are no more. Her eyes no longer see; the white veil of a forgotten history has covered them.

The *mecapal* clinging to her hips binds her to the only sign of life: the loom. Her body, twisted by the weight of nostalgia, forms the number two, recalling those who had and have no more. Sometimes when she remembers she's heard singing. Sometimes when she remembers she's heard speaking. But her singing and her voice vanish in the walls of the *cenote,* the sacred natural well, sealed by a pair of lips mutilated by the wrinkles of time and solitude.

Where does your journey end? Where does your desire take you? What tales do the hieroglyphics that mark your face lost in the darkness of weeping want to tell? One day a young archaeologist will come from afar and discover the forgotten treasure and offer it to the world. It will have to be a foreigner because the locals don't want to discover. It will have to be a foreigner because the residents don't want to hear. It will have to be a foreigner because the citizens see outwards with admiration and inwards with shame.

Oh, *abuela,* sing a song to me in Ixil! Don't let me fall asleep. Can't you see *las llamas me queman el sueño,* the flames burn my dream? Oh, *abuela,* tell me why two of everything and not one of nothing! You tell me, *abuela!* You who've been forgotten by history: why does history repeat itself? Why the scorched earth. Why the hatred for what we are! If you can hear me, my *estela Maya,* Mayan stelae, tell me of your 500 years of agony. Tell me that I didn't come in caravels but fogged in a dream in search of my lost roots. Tell me, I do want to listen....

Chapter 31
¡Por Lo Menos Escuchame, no Seas Culero!
At Least Hear Me Out, Don't be an Asshole!

Ishto kept running. He ran through tremulous streets that became treacherous alleys. He ran by *borrachines,* drunken men, lying on the sidewalk guarded by the fiery eyes of a dog. He fell several times but never stopped. He fell on asphalt. He fell on soil. He fell on shit but continued to pursue the past that had been hidden. His feet slid down a hill and his clothes were torn when the shrubs tried to restrain him not to follow. He fought back. He kept on running and when he could run no longer...he ran some more.

His desperation didn't let him notice that el Tripa once in a while turned his head to make sure he was still following them. He finally arrived at the place where they were going. It was a house, it was a small cave, it was a hut that stood simply because its walls were too lazy to collapse. Inside young people swung in the creeper of smoke from grass while others laughed with their nostrils wrapped in handkerchiefs soaked in something that splashed the whole place with its odor.

In one corner sounded the nervous laughter of a woman molested by a group of young men waiting for their turn; it segued to the crying of a man who had just remembered what he'd wanted to be when he grew up. A few empty beer bottles over here, human waste blended with yesterday's trash over there. Ishto walked between everything following the ringleader. The guards standing outside Tripa's room blocked his path but his simple loud whistle made them stepped aside.

La Seca, Tripa's girlfriend, hung herself from his neck. While she licked his right ear, she looked for the fruits of the night; she found only the package between his legs. He pushed her aside and she left *puteando,* cursing. She hadn't even see Ishto. She wasn't ugly but the abuses had marked her forever.

"I told you we were even. What else do you want?"

"I want the truth, Tripa. I know you know me, man!"

"Don't play fool! What the fuck do you want from me?"

"I don't know what happened to me, I don't remember anything."

"You're just fucking high and that's why you don't remember shit!"

"C'mon man! I know you know me. Please help me!" The name Tripa brought him comfort but he couldn't figure out why.

"Look, if you fucked up your head 'cuz of all the shit you fucking smoke or take, that's your problem *vos.* I don't fucking care so you either leave now or I beat the shit out of you!"

"*¡Por lo menos escuchame, no seas culero!* At least hear me out, don't be an asshole!" he shouted.

And he shouted as only an exasperated Guatemalan can. It was the first time ever that the *chapín* buried inside came out to retrieve his lost history. This cry sharp as an arrow finally tore the mantle covering the hole filled with the bats of forgotten time. Any other time, that would've been a person's last word. Tripa would've stabbed him with the knife hidden in his belt but something in the way Ishto had used that expression, so Guatemalan, so primal, showed him that this was a man lost in grief.

It takes one to see one. And he saw himself running alongside carrying the *jocotes* they had stolen before he'd even known him. And then he saw himself selling newspapers by his side, digging together through the garbage dump guarded by vultures, and shielding him from el Mono. Finally he saw himself telling him, *"Vos,* Ishto, why don't you go there? They know you over there. Maybe you can sell something. Those people are loaded and they always read the news and shit."

That had been the last time he'd seen him. He'd always blamed himself for not having protected him from the disaster. He'd loved him like a brother. Now fate was offering him something life and society had refused: a second chance. He looked him in the eyes and told him with the authority of a big brother, *"Sentate pues, vamos a hablar,* sit down, let's talk."

Chapter 32
It's Dawn Already and He Still Hasn't Come Back

"It's dawn already and he still hasn't come back, Pablo. What do we do?"

"The same thing we did when a comrade was late, remember? We sat around thinking of reasons why someone might be late so we would not go mad."

"Ay, Pablo, but there were so many times someone would come back to tell us that—"

"Pablo is right," Waldo said. "We can't jump to conclusions, plus that dude… Tripas…."

"Tripa," Tere corrected and sank onto the sofa barely breathing.

"Cool Tripa or whatever you wanna call him, he knows Ishto."

"How can he know him, Waldo? If Ishto doesn't even know who he is! Don't be dumb, please!"

"Boys, boys, calm down, we're all very stressed. Perhaps Waldo is right."

Kathy remembered how much she'd admired Pablo's analytical mind; it had conquered her from the moment they'd first met.

"If Ishto's parents," "Janis and Bob," Kathy said, "say that they found him here in the city, then it's possible he knew someone here."

"Yeah but you didn't see those guys," Tere said. "I got a really bad feeling about this. Those were thugs ready to—"

"OK, OK, let's not think the worse here, let's see…what did Ishto and that guy Tripa talk about?"

"I've heard that nickname before," Kathy whispered. "But where?"

"Well, they didn't talk much," Waldo said, "but they did talk about *la quemazón.*"

"What burning, Waldo?"

"Yeah, *la quemazón.*"

"When did they talk about that?" Tere demanded. "I don't remember anything about a burning, Waldo! Please don't make things up!"

"Yes, they did. Try to remember."

"How come you didn't say anything until now?" Kathy asked.

"Dunno." He was clearly embarrassed.

"Don't be too harsh on him, Kathy. The guy must of been all *ahuevado.*"

"Yeah, I was *ajuevado.*"

"Man is *ahuevado,* remember with a silent 'h', no *ajuevado.*"

"Well, whatever...what's that mean, anyway?"

"Freaked out," Pablo said.

"Well anyway, I remember 'cuz I was trying to forget about the damn knife sticking into my neck! Tripa said something about feeling bad for had left Ishto *en la quemazón.*"

"That must be the burning of the Embassy," Kathy said.

"Are you sure, man?" Pablo asked.

"I'll tell you, man, with a knife to you neck, a man must focus on anything other than that cold blade ready to cut his throat."

"By the way, we've got to take you to *la Cruz Roja*, Red Cross clinic. That knife might of been infected," Pablo said.

"So then they were friends and Ishto indeed was at the Embassy when it was taken," Kathy said.

"But how did he get out of there alive?" Pablo asked. "I thought only two people had survived that tragedy."

"Maybe he was there before the massacre."

"But then why the nightmares if he didn't live through it?" Waldo asked.

"Perhaps he managed to escape during the burning," Tere said, still lost in thought. "No, impossible. The windows were protected with metal bars."

"Well the good thing is that we think they know each other," Pablo said. "Maybe they're talking right now and Ishto is finally getting the answers he needs."

"I hope you're right, Pablo."

"Alright Waldo, let's go to *la Cruz Roja*, man. You need a tetanus shot."

"Does it hurt?"

"Nah. You won't feel a thing."

Chapter 33
He Kept on Dreaming...He Kept Remembering

By the time the light of the new day showed him where he ended up, Tripa had already told him everything he remembered about their friendship. It had not lasted more than a few weeks but it had bonded them forever.

Ishto had listened like someone would if a friend described the plot of a film he'd just seen. It moved him but he couldn't relate. At times he would remember a situation and would finish the story himself but most of the time it was like Tripa was talking about someone else. Exhausted from their journey through the past, they both had fallen asleep on *el petate*. And they had slept much like they had back when they'd fought to survive, keeping each other warm.

Outside the room the others tried to do the same but drugs blew the human warmth away from their bodies. While they slept, Ishto's cell phone bounced in the ravine he had crossed while searching for his story. Wrapped in the mist of the dream, reality took another form. He saw himself taking refuge behind Tripa when he'd fought for their little corner at el Mono's hut. There he saw himself running side by side with Cáscara fleeing *el Colocho* at the San Sebastián Park. In the dream everything was real.

Cáscara...what a nickname! Whatever happened to him? I've got to ask Tripa. So much lost in my mind. How did I come to the city? Where was I coming from? Perhaps if I went back to the bus depot.... But it would be impossible to find the owner of the truck that brought me here.

So many questions graffitied on the walls in the hallway of his mind and right in front of him Hamlet's dilemma. Why the fuck would I want to be when I don't even know who I am? Perhaps it would be better to just go home and forget about all this. He would never find his past. Too many questions left unanswered. He couldn't understand why, if he had left the Embassy before the fire, the event had affected him so deeply. He would never know the truth.

Perhaps he should just be grateful he hadn't ended up living with Tripa in this rotten underworld. Why keep hammering at his past? He had a life to live. He had Kathy, Tere and Waldo, and he had dragged them all along on this senseless search. They deserved better.

God, I almost got them kill because of my stupidity! I have pulled innocent people into this labyrinth. Nothing makes sense anymore. I just want to go home, I just want to forget. I want to thank my parents for giving me a life and taking me away from this filthiness. I want to thank them. It's done. I'm going home. To hell with this whole thing!

And covered with the blanket of determination, he kept on dreaming and kept remembering.

Chapter 34
To Rescue a Lost Story

With his buttock still swollen from the injection, Waldo fixed his sight on the ceiling illuminated in a perfect chiaroscuro. The soft light from the bedside lamp faded away like a youth's dream. To his right was an empty bed.

Ishto should be lying there, damn it! Listening to music, chatting about women, soccer, or anything at all, I don't care. I just want him here sharing our friendship.

He couldn't sleep. The demons of concern frightened his dream. Everyone in the house pretended to rest while waiting for news. He walked to Tere's room but didn't knock. The silence was better than the sound of the unknown. Up on the rooftop, the voices of Pablo and Kathy got lost in the choir of the wind whispering tales from far away and the flapping of fireflies playing at being shooting stars. He wasn't aware of their shared history but he sensed Pablo's happiness was in the red and Kathy was the only accountant who could put the books in order. On this night he felt irrelevant. He decided to flee through the window like a cat in heat to rescue a lost story.

Chapter 35
The Dream

As the sound of bongos filled the room, she clenched to her dancing partner as a moribund would his last breath. The fusion of sounds took them to a ritual on a Caribbean island where their bodies crashed into each other like waves against rocks. Amid the rhythm of the timbales, little by little the age difference diluted like the sweat of their faces dancing cheek to cheek. Little by little the twenty plus years sank into their throats that just wanted to swallow shared juice. Their tongues stirred sweat and saliva: key ingredients to the flavor of the mutual desire.

And while the frenzy continued, and while he tried to control the lack of dexterity of her mature body, she was happy in other dimension. How long would the adventure last? How long would this dream last? She didn't know and she didn't care. She'd already spent half her life worrying about the future while raising a son more or less the same age as this one who tonight swings her back and forth. The damn future, the damn tomorrow…her girlfriend, who worried so much about the future, had been buried this morning, leaving a beautiful daughter and a loving husband behind. Worrying about the future had been of no use to her. Her life had slipped away despite her worries. She won't do the same; right now she will care only about the present, which in moments would join the past.

They took a breather. He had a beer, they'd never heard of chardonnay here. He had an almost empty wallet; she pretended not to notice. She was laughing…she was enjoying…she was living the moment. They finally learned each other's names.

She gave him her first name only; he gave her the name that appeared on his ID. It was not the one his mother had chosen for him back home, though. They both showered themselves with liquor and returned to the dance floor. She was daring, he was daringly bold. They both pulled each other closer. They felt each other better. She felt him dark-skin, virile, erect, and masculine. He felt her dizzy, soft, and as white as the next page in his future, withered but with more desire to live than many of his past adventures.

They looked into each other's eyes: he saw the blue sky of his homeland and it took him to a place where he felt safe. She saw the darkness of an inviting cave. They both decided they would continue dancing while their clothes rested in a forgotten corner and fled the nightclub. From a dark corner someone witnessed the scene: two people lost in the fog of coincidence had found an anchor in the tempest of their truncated lives. The rich lady seeking in this cheap disco what she couldn't find in *la Zona Viva*.

"*¿Otra?* You want another one?" asked a girl who chewed gum as if yawning to life.
"No, thanks."
"OK. Have a good one then, 'cuz here those who don't consume are just in the way."
He gave her some money and left. The girl hid the bills in her bra wondering why he had given her money if she hadn't even flirted with him. Life had finally given her something for free.

They walked to a nearby half-star hotel. She paid for the room. The filthy key laughed at her French manicure. They made it to room number 3 *cuarto numero tres, por 'onde la querés*, the man at reception had rhymed while someone near the entrance pretended to negotiate with the girl showered by red light. The guy opened the door for her. Little by little he bought back his pride.

A chair, a table, a bed soaked by hidden passions and a lock that seals the deal. The intermittent red light winks and reveals the place in endless flashes. He was drinking the *Gaultier Classique* spilled on her flaccid neck while she felt the rough hands of this young immigrant touching the forbidden. She: a respected *señora*. He: a respected *soñador*. She with the lace of her Victoria's Secret *mojado*, wet. He wanting to someday become *un mojado más,* another wetback.

Clothes fell to the floor, high heels flew across the room, there was laughter, there was chaos, and they both gave in to desire. She started thinking about the excuse she would tell her companion in this convenient marriage while staring at the rising key that would open the door to much-needed ecstasy. He felt more macho than ever. She bit his dark nipples. He had to lower himself more than usual to find her delicate rosebuds.

On his way down in search of her pink lips that awaited him with wetness and anxiety, he left a little road of saliva on her belly carrying the extra weight of time. He finally arrived, kissed them, and from them enjoyed the nectar rolling down his jaw while preparing her to penetrate her story. She put a plastic package in his hand; he opened it with difficulty. She took him time after time to the very entrance of ecstasy but didn't allow him in until she wished. And when she finally did, the convulsion broke the dam restraining the milky river from the deepest of his wet and unsatisfied dreams. The protective bag barely contained its furry.

It was a night of frenzy; it was a night of learning. It was a night of pleasure; it was a night of unity. It lasted as long as it was supposed to...until the knock on the door vanquished the magic. Completely exhausted and drenched, they dressed while wishing for a pause button that would allow them to smell each other again. Their bodies left the room but later they would realize that something of theirs had been left beneath the wrinkled sheets.

They walked by the storyteller oblivious to his begging hand. They walked towards the main street while he told her he was just passing by Guate because he was going to *El Norte* in search of his mom. She told him that she too was searching for something she'd lost. She tried to give him some money but he refused it. She tried again, this time wiping her tears with the other hand. He took it, wiping his pride with the forearm of necessity. He hailed a cab and opened the door for the lady.

She continued living the night. And while she saw the world passing by through the window she smiled without guilt, satisfied, alive. She was a woman again. Tomorrow she would go back to the gym, revamp her outdated wardrobe, and keep on living.

He continued enjoying the night. And while he saw the world passing by as if nothing had happen, he got closer to the hard cold stone bench that would serve as bed at the bottom of *el Cerrito del Carmen*. Perhaps what had just happened had been a sign. Perhaps his future was here and not where he would find the woman who'd left him with his *abuelita*. He smiled. With the money this lady had given him, he could buy time and perhaps....

While he counted the bills, something fell. A man a few steps behind picked it up and caught up. The guy panicked. "I've got no money!" was the first thing he screamed.

"It's OK, dude, I just wanna give you something you dropped."

He eyed the stranger with mistrust.

"Be careful, man. Me and my friends just last night got robbed around here."

"Yeah, the city is getting dangerous."

They walked together for a bit. Waldo made a right and the other guy kept looking for a place to jump over the fence. Once in bed, covered by sheets of paper, Waldo started to write. Once in bed, with his jacket rolled up as a pillow the guy took one more look at the business card: *Diseños Beatriz. Beatriz de Posadas, Presidente.* At the bottom righthand corner in gold was a phone number. And he started to dream....

Chapter 36
Selective Amnesia

While they looked for a spot in the parking lot of one of the most important banks in the city, Kathy wondered whether it had been a good idea to leave Tere alone at Pablo's to wait for news from Ishto. Two days had passed since they'd last seen him, and serenity teetered at the edge to the abyss. They had traveled through downtown in a crab dance that would have tested anyone's patience: a little bit forward, a little bit sideways, step backward and forward again.

This was the city, a place with narrow streets that couldn't fit so many people and too many cars. The smoke from the public buses smudged the faces of waiting passengers. No one really knew when they would come or if ever and yet they had faith. Disorder was the order that move this metropolis.

"I'm worried. It's been two days, Pablo," she said

"Don't worry, I'm good at this. I promise you if something bad had happened, we'd know by now. You should of seen Waldo's face when they gave him the tetanus shot. *Puchica!* Jeez! He twisted his whole body."

Kathy started laughing. "I can't believe you didn't warn him...psycho."

"Today's youth need a little pain to get strong. What's that expression you guys have?"

"No pain, no gain."

"There you go."

"Men!" Kathy sighed. "Hey, so listen when did you start sleeping with the enemy?"

"*Jah!* Let me tell you about this guy. His story is so typical! He's a joke! You know, the rich kid who finds in the Left the way to show his rebellious side to his daddy but when things get sticky or he gets bored, he goes back to his parent's penthouse. That's exactly what happened. He works here." He pointed to a building hugged by sculpted stone murals that told a story no one wanted to decipher.

"He claims he graduated overseas. Just wait 'til you talk to him. You'll see he's a dumbass that doesn't know shit. He does look the part though but nothing else."

"And how can he help us?"

"Well, the thing is, he was involved in the planning of the taken of the embassy." He lowered his voice by instinct. This was still a touchy subject and even though he knew Kathy would never reveal their conversation, he was cautious. The city, after all, was full of ears. "And that's why his daddy shipped him overseas a few days after the tragedy. Of course once everything settled down, he showed up being an economist and all. What's that name people use nowadays?"

"Technocrat?"

"There you go."

They pressed the button marked *11* and by the time the doors opened up, they were already in another dimension: glass doors, beautiful wall-to-wall carpet, and dozens of employees fighting to be noticed by their boss.

"*El Licenciado* Posadas will be with you in a moment. Please take a seat."

When they entered his office, the view of the *Centro Cívico,* the Civic Center, took their breath away. Pablo wondered how it was possible to escape a country without leaving its border.

"It's called parallel worlds, Pablo, it's called parallel worlds," Kathy answered with the echo of a sigh.

"*Licenciado.*" Pablo put out his hand.

"*Pablo ¿cómo estás vos? ¿y ésta hermosa dama que te acompaña vos?*"

"This is Kathy Scarlet, an American scholar, a friend of mine."

"It's a pleasure to meet you," Posadas said in English to show off his knowledge of the language.

"*Gracias,*" Kathy responded.

They took a seat and told him everything. Francisco Posadas, Economist, as his golden plaque at the front of his desk read, looked at them the whole time. Then they showed him the picture of Ishto at the Capuchinas church in Antigua, the one Bob and Janis had taken the day they'd met him. Posadas recognized him instantly.

"Yes, indeed, *este patojo,* kid, walked with us from la San Carlos, *vos.* He was with Juan. I remember Juan because he was the only one I could communicate with. Almost no one else spoke Spanish, *vos.* To be honest with you, I don't think they fully understood what was going on."

"But do you know if he entered the building with the group?"

"I stayed outside, *vos,* but Juan did enter the building. *El patojo* must have too since Juan never let him out of his sight." As Posadas spoke, his hands caressed the leather-encased arms of his wine-red chair.

"I always wondered if *el patojo* was his little brother or something because he really took good care of him. That was horrible, *vos,* the flames coming out of the windows from the second floor. To hear the screams, the black smoke, the smell of gasoline and then see the burnt bodies when la Cruz Roja carried them out. I can't believe it didn't work. If they had just followed the plan to the letter."

Pablo wondered which plan. Oh, yeah, that's right! The piece of shit *Plan de la Subida* that told them how to get to the place but not how to get out alive. Which plan? The document that had been written in Spanish, a language they didn't understand. Which plan? The one on which the leaders listed how many pieces of fried chicken to order but not what steps to follow in case things didn't go as planned.

Or perhaps could have been that things had gone according to plan? Posadas the economist talked pretty but never mentioned his tendency to hide details. He suffered from selective amnesia. When things got ugly, he simply turned off the lights and didn't witness a thing. He was like that in everything. In commercial transactions, he omitted zeroes or hid facts that favored the other party.

And when everything else failed, he used his charisma to get away with it. He was handsome, refined, and he was well aware of it. That had been his modus operandi since he'd been a little boy. In his mansion many employees had lost their jobs because he omitted the fact that it was him who stole things from his parent's bedroom. And by the time he'd reached high school, with the technique perfected through practice, girls fell for the act. Now with a master's degree in omission, he decided not to mention that he had been the one who advised Juan to bring *el patojo* along to help their Cause. The Cause, yes! The new toy for the rich kid.

"Why did the leaders agree to bring a kid to the site? They knew it was dangerous!" Kathy asked.

"Huy los lideres...they were preoccupied with other things. I was not a leader."

No, of course not, Pablo thought. You've never been shit in your entire life.

"I just helped organize."

"But the media never said anything about a kid being there," Kathy said.

"Well, there was a photographer out there," Posadas said as he inspected his manicure. "He took some stills of the group and he knew about *el ishto.* We knew each other. I told him where we were going to protest so he could get better angles. You know how the media works. Besides, the pictures sold very well...in other countries, of course. Win-win. We used to hang out. Since he had his press credentials, he'd invite me to watch *partidos en el Mateo.* He'd be taking pictures and I'd be taking shots! *Mira vos,* we should go to el Mateo. The derby is coming up."

In the national derby: Pablo was red, Francisco was colorless. Kathy by now knew that, despite this man's refined mannerisms, he was not telling everything he knew.

"See, what happened was that once the *chontes,* the police, arrived and heard him say he'd taken pictures and that there was *un ishto* with them, they broke his camera. That was the thing with him. He talked too much, *vos.*"

"Can we talk to your friend?"

"Well, only if you guys know a good psychic, Kathy. They killed him soon after. I think they assumed he was part of the group since by selling pictures he was making the entire movement famous."

Poor Posadas. Now he was forgetting to say that by the time he got back to his parents' home scared shitless, a colonel displaying all his medals on his chest was waiting for him in the living room. They took him to his daddy's office and he recited everything including the *Ave Maria*. Why bother to say that it had been him who'd divulged the photographer's identity, who needless to say, ended up drowning in a tank of developer?

"Things got ugly after that, Kathy."

"I know. I was here."

"Oh, I didn't know you'd been here in the Eighties. Anyways I received a scholarship to study abroad and," he pointed to the diploma inside a beautiful frame, "with much regret I took it. OK, folks, that's all I know."

He stood up. "By the time the media heard about the invasion, many photographers and journalists arrived at the site but *el ishto,* if indeed he had gone inside.... I don't think anyone saw him after that. Besides, as you must know, the police fenced off the entire building. I heard they didn't let anyone near the ambassador's office on the second floor where the group took the hostages. I never heard anything about someone finding his body, though. But listen, I get off at four. If you want to join me for happy hour...."

He looked at Kathy.

"*Gracias vos* but we already got plans," Pablo said.

"Thank you very much, though," Kathy added.

"Perhaps some other time." He kept staring at her. "Here's my business card."

They left the office. The phone at the receptionist's office blinked and she ran to the office.

"Lock the door!"

She, knowing exactly what this call was about, let down her hair and knelt on the beautiful carpet. He leaned back while the ringtone of his cell announced a call from his wife. Her picture was released from the drawer only when his in-laws or his beloved wife visited. Why even bother to say that those beautiful blue eyes were burnt at the bottom of that drawer.

Chapter 37
And Together They Threaded History

To calm her nerves, Tere had gone up to the rooftop to sunbathe. It was such a placid afternoon and the sight of the beautiful *Cerrito del Carmen* spread out below could calm anyone. Birdsong traveled on the breeze that combed her hair across her shoulders. She has yet to visit the church at the zenith of the hill. She would do that later. She wanted to pray for Ishto's wellbeing. She closed her eyes. She wanted to think about nothing and ended up thinking about everything.

Downstairs Waldo was investigating the event. He wanted to look through the newspaper archive at the central library but leaving Tere alone now wouldn't be such a good idea. He loved her. He was now sure of it and was eager to reveal how he truly felt but this was not the right time. Then he wondered if the time would ever be right. Of course it would, he thought, but today was dedicated to research.

The Internet made everything easy. He just had to enter the name of the dictator and the date of the tragedy and Lycos would do the rest.... Bam! There were so many hits the screen looked like a war zone. He read whatever he found: official, decent, obscure, dirty, and even the funny sites. He learned that the dictator who used to live in the national palace, which now is known as *El Palacio de la Cultura,* The Cultural Palace, lives in Venezuela suffering from an advanced case of Alzheimer's disease.

He read and read and discovered that a Spaniard judge was preparing to prosecute the tyrant. He read and read and found out that he'd been the one who ordered armed forces to invade the Spaniard Embassy. He read and read and learned that the one in charge of executing the orders was possibly in the land of the Canal along with another who had left without paying the bill. He read and read until the bluish color of the computer screen stained his retina. His eyelids fell, and his forehead slowly collapsed beside the laptop. In that cyber limbo of zeros and ones, he walked with the muse disguised as HTML by his side and together they threaded history.

Chapter 38
God, Please! Take My Memory, Too!

He was lost in a television screen. There a president swimming in petroleum exchanged a bear hug with the one who'd come to power to liberate his people and who'd ended up enslaving them. He forgot what he'd just seen. His wife, his maid, his companion, his nurse, his everything brought a bowl of *atol blanco,* a hot drink made from corn flour, fixed just the way he liked: with *pepitoria,* ground dried pumpkin seeds, sprinkled on top and a cluster of black beans resting at the bottom. Would he still remember that this was the way he liked it?

He stared at the TV screen while his memory hit rewind and record, rewind and record, over and over and over in an endless repetition that made anything new and everything forgotten.

"Look," she says, "I brought you something to eat. You haven't eaten since this morning."
No answer.
"*Conchale vale,* why you keep looking at that? *Que aburrido!!* It's so boring!!"
Oh, Elsita! Poor Elisa! He used to call her that and now he no longer remembers. Can't you see that somewhere hidden in this surreal painting his memory has become, strokes still reveal the silly actions dictators perform for crowds outside the presidential palace? He, like many before him did, and now he enjoyed watching others do the same.

He tried scooping out a spoonful of *atol blanco* but his weak and shaky hand lost the route to his mouth and everything spilled. His flannel slippers sponged up some of the thick, sticky liquid. His companion in exile silently took the spoon from his trembling hand and fed him. Suddenly he punched her hand away.

He reached for the phone on a little table beside him and yelled with a voice that dragged in his throat, "What's happening? Why haven't you solved the issue...*Dejese de babosadas!* Solve the problem! I don't fucking care how, just get them out of there, just get them out of there! I said, I don't fucking care how, just get them out of there!"
The phone and the table went flying and a trail of *bip, bip, bip, bip,* bounced off the walls.
"*Por Dios!* Please come down," she cried. "You're going to hurt yourself!"

But he was no longer there nor was he agitated. He was watching the military parade in honor of the dictator's visit to the land of the *Libertador.* The woman left the bowl by his side thinking, hoping, he would eat something later. Deep inside though she knew that he had already forgotten what had happened. He wouldn't even remember that he'd been eating seconds ago. Much less would he remember that there had been a time when he'd offered his people *"un pan del tamaño de su hambre,"* a piece of bread the size of their hunger.

She cleaned up the mess and went to the other room to check the mail. There was a letter from Spain. She already knew what it was about but pretending not to, she opened it. A Spaniard judge was ordering a medical examination of the one lost in the flickering light of the TV. The Presidential anthems echoed around the house.

She wrinkled the letter in her right hand and drew it like a dagger to her heart. She imagined the circus of photographers, the flashes blinding her, the journalists shouting questions, the passionate recounts of those involved, the Nobel Peace Prize winner, the cries, the curses, the chaos, and he there in the middle of it all completely unaware. Weaken by the spectacle, she collapsed in the chair and let go a whisper wrapped in a prayer.

"God, please! Take my memory, too!"

Chapter 39
The Brilliant Puppeteers of the Politics of Terror

His life, his power, his luck and everything he had built crumbled that March 23. That day a group of military officers had changed the smirk but not the face of the government in a country that no longer had people to protest. He lived for a while afterward among palm trees but had finally settled at the 18th of Chiapas Street. He was happy there but an envelope from across the ocean had arrived to perturb his existence.

Fortunately he always walked one step ahead of everyone else. By the time the mess began in front of his house, he would already be on his way to the land of the Canal, Latin American's political brothel, the land where thugs were welcome as long as they had money to spend. On the road, he wondered how different his life would be if he possessed just a fraction of the power he'd claimed two decades earlier. He could fix the issue with just a phone call. He missed his partners on the other end of the line: Chupina Barahona, Valiente Téllez, García Arredondo, always willing, always hungry, so professional. The brilliant puppeteers of the politics of terror, well orchestrated, well synchronized. What a nice group they had assembled, how well they had served the regime doing what they did best.

Things were different now. Now he had to hide from everyone. Even from those up in *el Norte* who used to applaud his activities and provided him with the armament to contain the Red enemy. At every police checkpoint, he tossed money. He was glad to see that at least some things never changed. He closed his eyes for a moment and fragments of the past collapsed on the floor of his memory. The phone rang. It was he. He was furious. The entire world was watching this Centro-American capital.

"Who was in charge here, he or those *entierrados,* the filthy ones?"
"This is a delicate situation *señor Presidente,*" he tried to explain, "because according to International Law, the land occupied by an embassy is inviolable and I can't--"
"*Sho,* shut up," he grunted.
"But Cáceres Lehnhoff y Molina Orantes are insid.... Please verify the order--"
Click. Why wouldn't he wait? It was just a matter of time before they could have gotten to them. Why do it right there in front of the cameras? Things must be done accordingly. Stupid Bastard! That's why he got fucked in the ass and didn't even notice when they dropped his pants. He massaged his temples. I hope those *cerotes españoles,* piece of shit Spaniards, stop pushing the fucking extradition bullshit, he thought. Now they pretend to support and respect that fucking India! Now after they fucked as many as they wanted. Now they've all come out of the woodwork.... I wish Franco was alive! Then they'd shut up and put up. *Cerotes!* Where the fuck did I leave the aspirins? This fucking trip is giving me a headache.

Chapter 40
It's Your Destiny to Tell the World What Really Happened

"No, Ishto. You can't come back. Not just yet. I love you with all my heart son and I knew you were my son from the moment you hugged me ever so tightly seeking maternal love. I know you're hurting baby but you can't just ignore your duty. Your own blood is calling! You must find out what happened. You can't forget where you came from because if you do, you'd forget where you're going and you'd keep walking in circles."

"We love you very much Ishto, and we'll wait for you until you're ready to come back but you're not ready, honey. Listen, Bob and I have traveled a lot and even though we have enjoyed all those places and met amazing people, we've always come back to the States because this is our land. We've even joined demonstrations in front of our embassy whenever we thought it was necessary. We still complaint whenever the government violates our rights, and even though we're old now, we keep on doing it because this is who we are."

"We love the United States and we love the pure ideals that helped built this great nation. That's why we express ourselves whenever we think someone's attacking these ideals. I'm saying this honey 'cuz where we come from is part of who we are. And that must be the case for you, too. Your land is calling and you must answer that call. It's your destiny to tell the world what really happened."

"There will be a time for you to choose where home is but this is not the right time. You are not ready to come back. You were raised in the land of the free and the home of the brave, so don't let me down now..."

'le queda un minuto de comunicación en esta tarjeta telefónica...'

"...last thing I want is for you to someday find your biological parents and they think *que yo hacer mal trabajo en ti.*"

And she said it like that, using the wrong grammar but the right feeling. She used the language of his motherland to help him find the root that would attach him to this place: the place with the missing link.

"Mom, thank you for everything you've done for me. Thank you so much for taking me that day...and thank you for raising me and for waking up by my side after all those nightmares."

Tears trickled down his cheeks. The knot in his throat let through only a hiss drowned in a sigh. "I never told you this but...I wished with all my heart that I'd been born to you."

Janis dropped the phone. She tasted the salty rain her cloudy eyes proffered after the thunder of his simple phrase. She couldn't talk. She couldn't move. And through the tempest she again saw that little boy wearing a checkered shirt whose hair stunk like a sewer. He had fallen asleep immediately after clinging so tightly to her waist. She didn't say a word...she stood there feeling and nothing more. Nothing could destroy their bond.

Not the sharp edge of time or the flames that had burnt his childhood dreams.

"Ishto, it's me." Bob came on the line.

"Dad? What happened?"

"Nothing. It's just that...you just made your mother the happiest mother on earth. Take care, boy. Whatever happens, we'll wait for you. Good luck and--"

Bip...bip...bip...bip. That's how the conversation ended that afternoon when he'd returned to Juan Chapín to let them know he was coming home. Tripa was by his side. Almost everyone had tried to make him stay but no one succeeded except Janis. No one knew him the way she did. Despite what nature said...she was his mother and shared that bond.

He knew when she wasn't right. When she needed affection. And although they had never talked about it, he knew she had lost her unborn precious girl. They'd never said a word to him about the miscarriage but he'd found out. It had been the second time the stork hadn't finished her trip, and it would be the last time they would try.

Until now, he'd felt guilty about being jealous of his future sister. Now he realized how stupid it was to think that Janis' love would ever change. It was funny but now that he knew what he had in life, he felt the strength to look for what he'd lost. And lost in a world where the past played hide and seek, he was now traveling to the northern part of this land. At times the potholes dangerously mixed his volatile thoughts like a Molotov cocktail. Despite the danger, he kept thinking.

His sight was lost in the beautiful and exotic landscape surrounding the dusty road. The hilly mountains reminded him of the roller coaster ride his life had been on since he'd come back. To his left, Kathy slept leaning against his shoulder. Beside her sat Tere and lastly Waldo by the aisle...well, there wasn't really an aisle since people were standing. That was the way countryside buses operated. Waldo's left shoulder had become a kid's seat.

Whenever the bus passed by a transit checkpoint, those standing crouched down so the driver wouldn't have to pay the bribe for overloading. Kathy had seen this whenever she traveled to Latin America and was fine with it but to the rest it seemed dangerous. Istho was too lost in his thoughts to notice.

The dust of anguish applied a thin layer to Kathy's face. This was the first time she'd come to this area without a guide. She'd visited before with people who'd known which places to avoid. She still remembered the interview she'd conducted with Bishop Gerardi before the church closed the diocese of El Quiché. She had considered that an error, an abandonment, a betrayal... now it no longer mattered. To many not even the Case Gerardi mattered any more.

This time her visit was different and dangerous. She well knew that lifting stones around here was not a good idea, especially because one never knew what kind of worms hid underneath. She was completely puzzled by this whole thing. She believed the version Tripa had provided, especially now that Ishto had started to remember his life in the city. But why had Posadas lied when he'd said that he'd seen Ishto with Juan? Ishto didn't remember any Juan.

Posadas was not to be trusted but this time he had no reason to lie. Unless of course, he was just a pathological liar. Her friend Joan had finally reached David Stoll who'd helped her identify a family of a Juan who spoke Spanish, who used to live in Uspantán, and who'd been part of the group that had gone to the city and eventually to the embassy. That was their only clue. Maybe the kid Posadas had identified was not Ishto but just a family member...perhaps his brother?

Everything was so confusing. And of course there was a possibility that they both had been Ishto's brothers. But why would Juan have taken his own brother to such a dangerous place? The resemblance between them might be a coincidence. This after all was a pure race in which everyone looked alike.

So many thick branches sprouting questions whirled around this *Ceiba* of confusion. Deep inside Kathy knew that if they could find the trunk of the mother *Ceiba,* the tree that connected the underworld with the heavens, all their questions would be answered. But where did this *Ceiba* grow? Where stood this tree of life? They have walked on its branches without finding it.

She must rest. This had just begun. She would have loved to have Pablo by her side now but his father-in-law had grown ill and he'd been forced to go to Antigua. She would never admit it but she was happy that his wife had not been home when they arrived. Was it possible their shared story needed an epilogue?

Tere was so nervous. If she didn't love Ishto so dearly, she would've stayed in the city. She had been thrilled to learn Ishto was thinking about going home and had been furious when Kathy had suggested he call his parents for their opinion.

What does Kathy want? She had wondered. Why can't she see the pain this whole thing is causing Ishto? I'm sure she'll use this whole story to denounce the horrors of Rightist governments in Latin America from her lectern. I hope she doesn't do to Ishto what he must have done to Pablo. Tere was ready to fight for what she thought was hers.

By that point, Waldo had decided to help the father of the kid who had been sitting on his shoulder and who now sat in his lap. The way they both dressed was so peculiar, so colorful. All the indigenous people on the countryside bus, called *camioneta extra urbana,* dressed in ways dictated by the region they came from. Even their *caites,* their sandals, were similar, to help them distinguish each other. Those dressed alike got off the bus as a group.

He held the child on his lap until they reached *Los Encuentros.* The dad gave Waldo a *melcocha,* a sticky candy, some of which the kid had been eating the entire journey. By then the *melcocha* was all over his shirt and pants so he thought, why not? At first the mass stuck to his molars like clay. Once he started chewing, he discovered why the kid had never stopped eating it.

He offered some to his friends, still unable to completely open his mouth, but they waved him off. The priest sitting nearby told him they were near Chichi, the native reference for Chichicastenango. After spending the night there, they would venture to Uspantán and then.... *A saber*, who knows? A Guatemalan expression that refers to the unknown. Waldo had started building his own dictionary of *Guatemaltequismos*.

Chapter 41
Something Awaits Him There

From the moment they stepped outside the *camioneta,* they knew they were in another world. The cobblestone streets felt like they were walking along a dried riverbed.

"Come, you guys. I wanna show you something," Kathy said.

Soon they would arrive at the place where the river had been born. The night was dark but the wink from the moon provided enough light to illuminate their path. In this street, much like in life, it was difficult to advance. Their ankles tried to balance their bodies. Backpacks danced brusquely atop bodies unused to walking on streets outside the First World. A beautiful white church shaped like a *tinaja de barro,* an earthen jug, spilled its stones. This was the hidden birthplace of the cobbled river of forgotten conscience.

Even though it was deserted, they heard the noise of the market day. They smelled the incense that always follows the *cofradias,* the brotherhoods. And their eyes were lost in history detained. What could one do when he enters another dimension? What could one say when the foundation upholding the layers of time collapses and the past bypasses the present and the future goes on without waiting for its turn? The darkness penetrates the light and gives birth to shadows. The lie kidnaps the truth and hides it in a *costal,* a sack, of reasons. The water lights up the fire and make everyone tremble.

Your bother kills you to kill who he is. They insult you in their mother tongue because it is the only one they know. They change the way they dress to erase their history. They call you *indio* just to taste how it feels on the other side of the insult. You drop you head when they drive by in jeeps. You deny knowing him when they search for him. You pray for *Tata Dios* to smack him on the back of his head so he will understand that he shouldn't be trying to change things. Everyone has his own destiny, and when one tries to change it, the soil opens up and swallows him.

This was how don Nicolás had described Juan when they'd found him in Uspantán. "When we saw the pictures in the newspaper the first of February, we didn't know what to do. That day we swallowed our tongues and talked no more. Then *el ejercito,* the army, came and recruited *patojos* for the *Patrullas de Autodefensa Civil,* Civilian Self-Defense Patrols. That was when we really started destroying our own selves, *seño.*

"No, *señorita,* miss, he didn't have any *hermanos,* brothers. Her mother dried out after he was born. I think that's why he liked being around friends. That's how they filled his head with those *babosadas,* crazy ideas, *seño.* And when he started teaching Spanish, they called him a traitor. But he just wanted to help. He loved helping kids. You know, when he learned what had happened in Chajul, he took care of one of the poor *patojos* who'd survived.

"Yes, *seño,* this is him. Where did you get this picture? *Hay Dios,* it's been so long since I last saw him but yes, this is the *patojo* that was with Juan. I don't know what happened to him because after Juan left with don Vicente, we stopped seeing him around. I did tell Juan, 'You've better not get this *patojo* in any trouble 'cuz remember his poor *abuela* already suffered enough.' Yes, *seño,* the poor woman lost his mind after she lost the first one, this one's bother. The one from your picture.

"Believe me, *seño,* even through the spiderweb I can still see. They were *igualitos,* identical, like the two brothers from the legend, you know. *Oiga,* listen, *seño,* why are you asking all those questions *pues?*"

Kathy left a *muchísimas gracias,* thank you very much, bouncing off the walls of the *rancho* before she and Waldo ran to tell Ishto. The three of them had agreed it would be best for him not to see Juan's *abuelo*, grandpa. Tere would keep him busy then they would all meet by the church in the central plaza.
"The poor thing is so happy we found a clue," Kathy said, "if this ends up being a dead end it would be best if friends break the news."

Ironically, they gathered at the same place the *campesinos,* the peasants, had planned their trip to the city. This group of friends, like the group from decades ago, had judged this the right place to start the beginning of the end. Waldo couldn't believe Ishto's twin brother had died in an event that had forever marked Guatemalans.

"What are we gonna do, Kathy?" he asked.
"We tell him the truth, Waldo. Then we go to Chajul. Even though don Nicolás doesn't know if Ishto's *abuela* still lives, I have a feeling that something awaits him there."

Chapter 42
La Abuela Didn't Finish Her *Tejido,* Textile

La abuela didn't finish her *tejido,* textile.
La abuela, who for the very first time had
embroidered two *quetzales* facing each other on
each side of a *ceiba,* stopped and wove no more.
She remained curled up waiting. Time forgot her.
The neighbors forgot her. And while the waters
from the river kept running, the waiting grew tired
of waiting.

Abre los ojos abuela que tu nieto te espera.
Open your eyes grandmother, that your grandchild
comes no further. *Abre los ojos vieja que tu dolor
ya te deja.* Open your eyes you old woman, and
share your pain with that young man.

"God, please don't take me. I must wait for
the one who is coming to see me."

"No. Your destiny has ended. Come. Your
husband, your son, your daughter-in-law and
grandchild want to tell you all about living in the
milpa divina, the divine cornfield."

"*Hay mi señor,* oh God, please! I served
you. I took everything you sent my way. For over
five hundred years they have violated us. Please
just give me a little breath to feel him. Let him lull
me in his arms the way I used to lull him. Let him
find his burnt history."

"You old fool! Don't you see that what is
written must be obeyed!"

"Please, God, give me more pain if that's
what it takes. Give me more suffering but please
don't take me now that I feel him coming."

"*Abuela Ixcanil,* come. See, here's *Tata,* grandpa, I'm here with everyone else. Come, *abuela,* let's play with the blowpipe."

"Please, my Creator, please! He just arrived in town. He's asking for me now; he's so close now."

"If you don't come now, you will stay here with no body and no life."

"Please, God, look at him. The poor thing is tripping all over. Look, he busted his knee, my little child. Look, God. He just remembered when he rolled me out of the burning hut. Please, God, let me stay for a little bit. Look, he just remembered when we used to play in the river. Look, he just remembered when I used to take him to see you at church. *Seré tu esclava. Seré tu sierva fiel.* I will be your slave. I will be your faithful servant."

"Well, if that's what you want."

Thunder was heard.

"Stay lost in the nothingness."

"*Abuela,* please come. We are waiting for you."

"No. It is too late now. Let the doors be closed. She made her choice."

When Ishto stepped into the hut, he found *la estela Maya,* Mayan stela hunched like a hieroglyphic before the unfinished textile. He fell to the floor and his groan reached the heavens and burst the *tinaja* holding the water. It started to rain. The cry from the heavens slammed into the hut without mercy. The pieces of the broken *tinaja* fell like thunder in the mountains and a river washed the cobblestone outside. The rain lashed the hut where Ishto finally remembered everything.

"Abuelita Ixcanil, abuelita Ixcanil, why didn't you wait for me? Why so close and yet so far away?"

He lifted her and carried her outside. He ran up to the mountains; the unfinished textile wrapped them both. The entire pueblo followed them among the thunder and lightning. The darkness became night and the rain was as salty as tears. The ghosts cried. Someone had made a mistake. Ishto made it to the zenith of the mountain and fell to the ground with his *abuela* in his arms.

The loose threads of the textile penetrated the soil. They wormed deeper and deeper looking for the blessed *savia,* sap from a mass grave. The two *quetzales* in the textile fought to be free. The *Ceiba* ripped the textile. The ceremony had begun. Incense and candles burned around them to illuminate the birth of *Yaxché,* the sacred tree of life.

In the midst of the ceremony, he and his *abuela,* he and his history once again became lost in reality. The Mayan priest sang, danced, and spit on the ground knowing he had power to reunite these two in another dimension. He drank from a vessel and levitated until he reached Ishto with the lifeless body of his *abuela,* and he spilled on their mouths the light of truth. From his mouth came smoke, voices speaking in other tongues.

The smoke surrounded them, and from the smoke the tree grew and its branches carried them into the heavens. They swung from the *quetzales'* tails. The air was filled with sacred incense. From above they watched the priest offering his heart to the gods.

"Oh, my child, I waited for you as long as I could. Your bother, la María, your mom and your dad are waiting for you. I no longer can go because I disobeyed Tzacol and Bitol. I will remain here between the nothing and the everything. When your time arrives, you will be reunited."

"*Hay abuela no me dejes,* please don't leave me. I want to understand. Tell me what happened. Why they kill us? Why they hunt us?"

"I don't know, my precious child. Go ask those who live. Now I must go to wander in the nothingness. I accept condemnation for my rebellion. Send me, my Creator, to the never-ending field."

"No, *abuela no me dejes,* please don't leave me!"

"I always prayed to see you again and now that you've come back the prophecy has been fulfilled. Now I leave happy."

"Please tell me about my brother. What happened to him?"

"If you want to know, you must go through the wall of flames. Face your fears, my beautiful child; face your destiny, my beloved kid. Go look for your brother. Go get what the fire took from you. I have accomplished what was required of me. Now it is your turn."

A cloud rose from beneath her and carried her to the sacred cornfield. There she saw her husband, her son, her grandchild and her daughter-in-law.

"I don't understand, God."

"The Mayan priest took your place, you stubborn old woman."

Ishto was once again alone. He began to sweat, to tremble. A wall of fire, a wall of flames stood before him challenging. He knew then what he must do. He ran towards them. He ran as hard as he could and jumped through.

His brother is hunched in a corner. A man dressed in a dark suit negotiates through a door blocked with chairs, furniture and whatever else they'd found in that office. Juan, his face covered with a handkerchief, protects him with his body. From inside, men in business suits use a megaphone to plead for calm. His brother is crying. Everyone shouts. Out in the hallway, they try to break the door down.

Inside the room, a bottle hits the door. Liquid spills down to the floor. The ceremony begins. The bottle doesn't blast into an explosion. Someone tosses a match. The one near the door controls the fire. He begs those in the hallway. Someone in the room is holding his arm. Nobody listens. Inside the office everyone screams; outside everyone shouts. They pound at the door.

In the confusion... a blast. The door catches fire. The flames lick the man in the dark suit before he escapes through the door. The fire burns. Everyone screams. Gunshots. The four who dressed differently than the rest of the group, the priests of this damned ceremony, the ones offering the sacrificial lamps, those who covered their faces with red bandanas with a white star patch embroidered on the center, step in front of the door. The gunshots continue.

"No hay redención sin dolor," someone announces, "there is no redemption without pain."

The machetes burn. Juan lifts him up so he could breathe. Everything burns, smoke clouds over, heat cooks their bodies. From the window, a breath of heat blows at the face of a beautiful day. The screams, the explosions continue. Men, women, everyone writhes in the flames with Tohil in the middle of it dancing to the sacrifice. The flames finally reach the window now the bars burn.

Through the flames the child spots his brother standing across the street. The boy outside screams. He runs to the gate. He'll climb to the second floor and rescue his other half. A man from the *Pelotón Modelo,* the police, grabs him and tosses him to the ground. He can't stand it anymore. He feels the flames burning his body.

"He must be high," a woman says as the child twists on the ground. She entertains herself watching the holocaust.

The explosions continue inside. Ishto starts to run. Tripa and Cáscara watch everything from the opposite corner: the fire, the black smoke, the chaos. Tripa screams "Ishto" and Cáscara grabs him to keep him from moving any closer. More flames. A gunshot. And Ishto ran and ran. Behind him everyone took pictures. And Ishto ran and ran. The firemen tried to contain the flames. And Ishto ran and ran. Someone called the president: *Misión cumplida,* Mission accomplished. And Ishto ran and ran. The group members who'd stayed outside leave before someone started asking questions. And Ishto ran and ran. Posadas had already left. And Ishto ran and ran. The evidence that a child had been there will be erased. And Ishto ran and ran. At the end the bodies were disfigured, the chemicals petrified them. And Ishto ran and ran. Tohil satisfied gathered those who belong to him. And Ishto ran and ran. They would not let Gregorio speak. And Ishto ran and ran. The ambassador will be slandered.

Y finalment la nube negra tizna al sol, and finally a black cloud blows on the sun. Now the ceremony has concluded.

Dodging through the legs of the crowd, Ishto climbs on the bus. *"Ishto mierda!* You little piece of shit!" a woman screamed.

He finds Janis as Bob struggles to store their backpacks in the overhead compartment. Ishto collapses, completely exhausted and without memory. That woman would become his mother. He had been reborn.

Chapter 43
And From the Ashes His Conscience was Born

He gently packed all the textiles his *abuela* wove in a suitcase. The last one was still in the ground at the mountain's zenith. A beautiful *Ceiba* hid the secret of what happened. The dream finally burned, and from the ashes his conscience was born.

Tere is already in the States finding jobs for them and Kathy is helping the village obtain drinking water. The *abuela* enjoys life with her family in the sacred cornfield. The love of the *abuela* changed the Creator's mind and the Mayan priest's sacrifice maintained the universal balance. Sometimes what has been written must be edited. Once in a while the *abuela* will escape in the form of an eagle, a dove or even a squirrel to see her *nieto,* her grandchild and his *Nahual* will always be with him.

Waldo, sitting in the shade of the *Yaxché,* has not stopped writing since Ishto regained his memory. Since that day, his only food of inspiration has been fruit the tree drops by his side. No one would ever have the heart to tell him that this was a gymnosperm. And the fool would think he and no one else created the story that, if I remember correctly, started something like this:

A dark thick cloud obscures his vision and scorches his throat. He swallows smoke. He swallows sorrow. He swallows his own memory immersed in the gush of salty water dripping from his forehead that carries desperate shouts....

Epilogue

After the TV interview, which by the way went very well, they even called me an "up and coming Central American writer." I managed to escape Cesar, my editor. I just wanted to be alone, away from everyone. I don't mind criticism but I must admit it hurt me when some people thought I had written this novel to benefit a specific group from the political spectrum. But I do accept the fact that the moment one ventures to reveal a novel or any other piece of art, approval as well as disapproval must be accepted.

I'm glad I decided not to ask Ishto to join me on this promotional tour. He would have supported it but it wouldn't have been right for me to ask. The important thing is that he liked the story. Honestly, I wrote it for him and to humanize the facts. Rooted by that *Ceiba* which hides our secret. I still remember his eyes, bloody red, just like his brother's must had been that afternoon on January 31.

In the silence of my room on the eleventh floor of this hotel that provides a view of the *capital chapina,* the Guatemalan capital, I change into a pair of worn jeans and black t-shirt that fits as nicely as a longtime girlfriend. I gather up my wallet and my cell phone to stay connected along with a bottle of filtered water. I leave to pay tribute to those who have become objects of manipulation by political interests. The red light in the land phone winks at me but I pay no attention.

I'm gonna get lost. But I'm not worried. Those who have found themselves will always find the place they wish to be. While I drive further and further from the city, a question mark hangs like an earring from my left ear. What is the duty of the Latin American novelist? Is it fair to write about someone else's pain? Would it be possible that I too am exploiting the victims of this horrible tragedy? Or is it possible perhaps that I am betraying the real people involved by manipulating them to make the narrative flow?

It is so difficult to find the balance between reality and fiction, between exposition and metaphor. That simple phrase sneaked into the car as I finally left the world of the city behind. And it was then that I understood there is no such thing as an absolute history. Before I found a publishing house willing to publish my novel--some even suggested I should add a religious component since that was selling well at the time while others advised me to copy the classics--I researched so much about the Spanish embassy affair I decided to change the narrative altogether. When I showed Ishto the new draft, he threw it in my face.

"Let me ask you something, *vos*. Are you a novelist or a historian?"
"A novelist."
"Well, then do your fucking job. And if you don't have the balls, don't even try."
And I returned to the original draft.

It's amazing how Guatemala changes when one climbs on the back of this animal drained by the damned usual ticks. The cool air from the mountain slaps my face and wakes me from the existential anxieties that have always color my dreams. Without noticing, I remember a paragraph I wrote for one of my literature courses at AU when the watch scratched out the third hour of a new day and the last drops of the red wine stained the bottom of a bottle. My fingers stroked the keys of my laptop with the ease of the one who, being drunk, no longer cares to hide what he really thinks. I wrote something like

...with the emergence of the post-modern novel, books that merely entertain were left behind. While it is true that the post-modern novelist still seeks to entertain, they also try to inform. Above all, they invite readers to participate not only in the plot but also in the real facts that inspired the work. There is no room for pure fiction. Now the writer asks the reader to become part of the social change. The Latin American writer uses historical facts to legitimize their characters, to show the impact on them and on real people. In this way they construct "the new Latin American history."

The most important element in this new type of literature is the reader. The one who reads and doesn't stop there. The one who investigates, the one whose curiosity is challenged by the writer. The one who believes we are all responsible for a better future. The writer knows that without the reader as an active accomplice, the search for a better tomorrow will be impossible. That is why each new novel shouts a new invitation.

Now it is up to you to accept it. You who read, think, and do not settle merely to exist, and who wants to become active participate of this great Latin American history that until this moment has been denied and now needs to finally start living.

I was surprised that I remembered it word for word. That paragraph hit me like waves striking rocks by the levee and washed away my doubts. Suddenly I in my own past had found the answer to my tribulations. At least as far as my role as a writer, ha ha. Now I know that I don't have to explain why I write to anyone. The only thing I must do is send the invitation to accompany me in the search not for facts but for how they affected the lives of those who lived them.

My two stretching breaks, Chichi and Santa Cruz del Quiché, were left behind. I entered Uspantán and the first thing I do was buy flowers. I felt at home. When one suffers or sees a loved one suffering, that place becomes as familiar as home. I asked for the monument.

Don Manuel said, *"Sígale derechito joven,* just keep going straight, boy. It's near the school. It's simple. Don't expect a huge thing. We just wanted to do something to remember those poor souls. You'll see it. It's a cement stone with a cross and their names."

The monument is exactly as don Manuel described. I was tempted to create a metaphor from the whole experience but as soon as I saw the monument, I undressed myself of the profession. Once naked, I was a simple man paying tribute to some of the victims of a devastated civil war.

Lost in my anxiety, I didn't realize that someone had followed me. Even I who brag about being a full-time observer had become one who goes through life without paying attention because of my internal fight. While I positioned the flowers that smelled like hope, a fat, bold man hunched by the weight of history he carried on his shoulders much like the bundle of sticks kids carry with a *mecapal* as they clip up the Cuchumatanes mountain approached.

"I saw you this morning," he said.
I thought he was a fan. Fan! What an idiot! Just one novel out and I already think I have fans.
"*Perdón,* excuse me?" I said the way people do when they are buying time to understand the situation.
"On the TV," he added. "I also listened to the radio interview yesterday. You know...you didn't tell the whole story."
"That was not my intention, don...?" I opened the door for an introduction but he remained at the threshold.
"It'd be better if everyone just forgot. That's what people should do. When they look and look at the wound, it never heals."
"That's easy to say when you're not the one who's bleeding."
"*Vos no sabés nada, nada,* you know nothing, nothing at all."
"Well, why don't you tell me, then?"
He looked at me like a child spying a jar of cookies. He looked at me as one who knows the truth would set him free. That was the first time he'd looked at me. Up until then, he'd stared at the monument adorned by my flowers.
"Nah," he said. "There's no use."
"But--". I began but it was too late.

He left like a wounded animal, trying to salvage some dignity knowing that this one had been damaged on the battlefield. He climbed into his car and left. A couple of women lost in age walked by, and I asked them just to make sure the man had not been one of my fictional characters burped out by my imagination.
"*Disculpen señoras.*"

"Señoritas," they corrected.

"Pardon me. Did you see that man I was talking to?"

They gazed at me strangely. They must have thought I was crazy. "Of course, young man. Wasn't he just talking to you? Besides, he always comes here. *Vámonos Panchita,* let's go, Panchita."

The oldest took her friend by the arm. As they walked away, she kept looking back. I laughed because even though they must have thought I was crazy, their answer had proved I wasn't.

As I started the car, I found a manila envelope on the passenger's seat.

I opened it with the curiosity of the *buscador de historias,* the stories hunter. Inside was an old picture. It showed the man I had just spoken to twenty-five years earlier on the day of the massacre. He stood outside the embassy wearing his light blue shirt uniform carrying something that looked like a *lanzador de llamas,* a flame thrower, or one of those *lanzador de niebla paralizante,* a paralyzing fog throwers. The chemicals are extremely irritating to the skin, almost petrifying. What was he trying to tell me? I held the picture while the car lulled my subconscious. I said to myself... Here's a story to tell.